No W

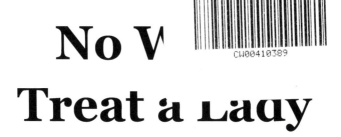

CW00410389

Treat a Lady

A Contemporary Romance

Based on a True Story

By

J K Ashley

Note from the Author

This was a very moving and emotional story to write as it was based on a real-life situation with a lot of explicit detailed action that could possibly relate to other people.

Editorial Review

A wonderful writer skilled at creating characters that are realistic and unique. I love editing her books. She creates masterful suspense every time that keeps me on the edge of my seat, rooting aloud for her characters as they face dangerous and unpredictable situations

Marie

Short Summery

When Jane first began dating James Harman she was smitten and head over heels in love. When he finally proposed to her she really imagined that all her dreams had come true. He was perfect. He was wealthy, owned substantial land and was very handsome. What's more, her parents liked him too. It was the ideal match for the fun loving and bright young woman.

Being a virgin on her wedding night, Jane envisaged a beautiful romantic experience. But her world was abruptly shattered when her new husband revealed his true nature as she experienced his brutal penchant for violence, abusing her both physically and mentally.

As James' controlling nature takes an ever-greater hold of her life, Jane searches for a way out of the relationship. Fear of the consequences forces her to stay with him, but then one evening, at a dinner dance, she meets the dashing Captain Phillips and suddenly finds that she has feelings she never knew existed.

With James' in the background, his brooding jealousy dictating everything that happens in her life, will Jane find the courage to be rid of him for good? And is Captain Phillips the man for her, or is he just a welcome distraction from the relentless domestic violence she faces?

A Very Emotional Love Story based on true events intended for the mature reader.

CONTENTS

Chapter One

Both my parents liked James and frequently suggested that should he offer his hand in marriage. They said that I would be foolish to turn him down as I may not get another opportunity. So naturally they were delighted at the news of our engagement. Their excitement was increased since he owned a large manor on a 100-acre estate in Kent near London that housed a large stable block and many more outbuildings. He was a very rich and successful business man in the textile trade but more importantly he always acted like a perfect gentleman and treated me like a lady.

We decided to get married on my 26th birthday at the local village church and the reception would be held at the Grand Hotel just two miles away. After all the necessary preparations, the big day arrived. It was a glorious sunny day and I was feeling both nervous and excited as the horse drawn carriage pulled up outside the church. With the help of the bridesmaids holding the train of my dress, I stepped down from the carriage. As we entered the church the organ began to play as my father came over to escort me down the aisle to where James was waiting. He looked immaculate and so very handsome in his dark pin-striped suit.

It had been a long but perfect day and after saying our goodbyes, James and I left for our honey moon, leaving our family and friends to continue enjoying the rest of the evening. We drove to the airport and after checking in we boarded our flight destined for the romantic city of Venice. On arrival, an awaiting taxi took us to our hotel where we were greeted by a friendly porter who carried in our luggage. After a warm welcome from the desk staff we signed in and then were given the key to the honeymoon suite. The porter organised our luggage and escorted us to our room. On entering it was quite magnificent with low lights and scented candles. After thanking the porter and giving a generous tip, we were finally on our own.

It was 11.00 pm. After enjoying a glass of complimentary champagne, I unpacked my nightwear and went to the bathroom to get ready for our first intimate night together. I put on my new nightdress that I bought for this special moment. I so wanted to look desirable and pleasing to him, as this was the night I would lose my virginity. After a final check in the mirror and a small spray of my favourite perfume, I nervously made my way out of the bathroom and into the bedroom where James was standing by the bed in his black silk dressing gown.

I went over to embrace him and spoke in a soft

tone, "You know this is my first time darling as I've kept myself only for the man I would marry. I am now yours so please be gentle with me."

He leaned towards me as if he were going to kiss me, but then stood back and had a strange look in his eyes. "So, you're a virgin and want me to be gentle with you, but as you quite rightly say you are now mine, so let me make one thing perfectly clear. From here on in we do things my way and my way only." With that said he put his arm forward, ripped off my nightwear and threw my naked body onto the bed. I was so shocked as it all happened so quickly and unexpectedly.

"Please James don't hurt me. I'm not sure what you want me to do." He just stood there with a big smirk on his face then took off his dressing gown, bearing his naked body that was boasting his erection and I knew one thing for sure, this was going to be bloody painful. He came over, stood by the bed, and looked down at me.

"I've waited a long time for this moment, it's now my pleasure to make a real woman out of you." He got onto the bed and knelt over my naked body. I could feel his shaft touching my inner thighs searching for my opening. My whole body tensed as he tried to enter me then with one powerful thrust he forced the full length deep inside me.

I cried out, "Please stop James! You're hurting me." But the more I cried out the harder he fucked me. My resistance seemed to turn him on and I was powerless to stop him. Although the pain was immense, thankfully it was only for a short while. His body arched as with one final thrust and he released himself inside me. After he had finished I ran crying to the bathroom. Not surprised to see that I was bleeding, I decided to have a shower and cleanse myself. After a long and comforting shower, I felt refreshed and a bit more relaxed but was still shaking and feeling very sore.

I left the bathroom and nervously made my way over to the bed only to find him out cold and snoring like a pig. Still in tears and feeling somewhat sad and bewildered, I sat on the edge of the bed trying to figure out why he had treated me in such a brutal way. I was expecting something very special and romantic on our wedding night and not to be abused in such a physical way. Being a virgin, I thought that perhaps it was my fault since I didn't have any sexual experience and could please him, although he gave me no opportunity to do so. I always thought that men were proud to have a woman that was pure and innocent in that way. James had always treated me like a lady and I always thought of him as a kind and considerate man. But I have now seen a very dark side of him, one I had not seen before or ever imagined. One that makes me feel deeply hurt and concerned.

After only a few hours' sleep I awoke only to see James come from the bathroom fully dressed. He came over towards me and smiled.

"Come on then, get yourself up darling. It's time we went down for breakfast." I couldn't believe this was the same man who had just treated me so badly on our wedding night, now acting as though nothing was wrong.

"James, please tell me why were you so cruel and horrid to me on our first night together?" He came back over to the bed and scowled at me. "So, you got fucked and lost your virginity and yes it may have hurt but what did you expect? Sex is going to happen on a regular basis so get used to it and in time you may even get to enjoy it. By the way, as I recall in church and as was witnessed by all in attendance, you quite clearly stated entirely of your own free will these words 'I promise to love, honour and obey you till death us do part,' So what is your problem?" Feeling myself well up with emotion I went to the bathroom to get dressed, as I emerged I was greeted with,

"About bloody time, if you're going to take that amount of time just to get dressed, then tomorrow I'll go on down without you," Having arrived at the dining room we were greeted by the waitress and shown to our table. With breakfast over I turned towards James and spoke in a gentle tone,

"Have you any plans for today, perhaps to visit somewhere of interest?" He looked at me as if I had said something stupid. "I'm not into sight- seeing but as it's such a grand day and the local golf course is at hand I think I'll go down and have a few rounds. You on the other hand can do what all women like doing best—going off on a shopping spree. I'll catch up with you later this afternoon." This wasn't the honeymoon I or indeed any other woman could ever envision for their selves. It was more like a bloody nightmare. The rest of the week carried on in very much the same vein. Every day he played golf and at night used my body for his own gratification with total disregard for my feelings or emotions.

Chapter Two

After the so-called honeymoon, we left Venice. On arriving back home were greeted by my parents, who had come over to welcome us back. We gave each other a hug and then went inside, my mother of course being my mother was keen to know how the honeymoon went.

"So how was Venice?" Before anyone else could say a word, James spoke out, "Venice was absolutely amazing. Such a romantic place wasn't it darling? We just had the most wonderful time and we were sad to leave." He then looked at me in such a way as if to say. "Do not dare disagree with me", both my parents were happy in their belief that we had such a great time and after tea they departed.

James went in the dining room to make a phone call. I went upstairs to unpack, and a few moments later there was a knock at the door. It was the house maid.

"Excuse me Milady is there anything I can get you?"

"No thank you Edna, not at this moment in time but perhaps you would take these clothes to the laundry room and kindly inform me when they're ready." With that she took the garments and left. Edna is a very nice lady and I know we will get on well together. After a long day, James and I retired and went up to bed. This was our first night together in my new home and I wasn't quite sure what to expect. As we were getting into our nightwear James came over to me.

"Tomorrow I'm away on business and will be away for a few days. On my return I, will expect everything to have been in order, such as making sure the day-to-day chores are taken care of as it is now your duty to delegate the staff for the appropriate work. I will be leaving in the early hours. So as not to disturb you, I will on this occasion be sleeping in the adjoining room and will next see you on my return in two days' time." So, on our first night in at the new house he was sleeping in the next room. I wasn't disappointed. *At last I thought, I may get a good night's sleep and give my body a chance to recover. I'm already having mixed feelings about this marriage but I must give it a fair chance as it could just be my fault not knowing what a man wants or how to please him. After all, I've had zero experience in this area. And I know my mother would say, "You've made your bed now lie in it."*

I really wanted to make it work and would endeavour to do so. I wasn't very sleepy so I decided to have a read. Just as I was getting cosy I heard the bedroom door click. I looked up to see

James' tall figure walking towards me. As he got to the bed I folded back the sheets in a gesture for him to join me, and I smiled up at him.

"Hi darling, are you going to spend the night with me? It would be so nice if you would." He dropped his dressing gown and leaned over me. "Turn over I've got something for you." I turned over onto my stomach and then felt his hand go between my thighs. I could feel lubricant on his fingers as he began to insert them deep inside me. Perhaps this was going to be different, foreplay. He then got on the bed and took me from behind. Upon him entering me I winced in pain, but was no longer going to cry out as this only spurns him on to hurt me even more. After relieving himself he got off the bed and left the room without so much as saying a word.

Although not experienced in this department, I felt sure he must have a problem as he can only manage it for less than a minute. But at this moment in time I was truly grateful as it minimised the enduring pain. Surely there must be more to a sexual relationship than this. I envisaged sex being something wonderful, loving and a passionate experience. *Perhaps as we spend more time together things will change.* I truly hoped so, as I really wanted to make this marriage work but felt we both had to make the commitment. Not in the mood for reading, I just lay here thinking, *what the bloody hell is going on?* I was feeling totally confused, not sure as to what my role was in this relationship.

It's 8.00 in the morning, time for a shower then to find something casual to wear. After breakfast I was going to visit my mother and have a chat with her. I didn't want to go into too much detail but hoped I may pick up a bit of advice as she has been with my father for over thirty-five years. Before leaving I just checked to verify that James had left as nothing would surprise me anymore, especially at this point

After a short drive, I arrived at my mother's. She was sat in the drawing room reading in front of a lovely open log fire.

"Hello mother." She put down her book and turned towards me. "Hello Jane my darling nice to see you. Would you like a nice cup of tea?"

"Yes, that would be wonderful." She rang the bell and requested the house keeper to bring tea and biscuits. I went over and sat in the chair opposite hers.

"So, what brings you over to see me? I'm sure it's not for tea." She sat back in her chair with a curious look, awaiting my reply. Before I could say anything, the maid knocked on the door and brought in the tea.

"Put the tray down there," she said, pointing to the small table beside her. She poured the tea and passed one a cup to me together with a small plate of biscuits and then turned her attention once more towards me.

"Come on then darling, out with it. What's on your mind? Something is troubling you and don't say there isn't as this is your mother you're talking to." I know she's my mother but I wasn't sure as to how far I should go in asking for advice on how one is to conduct oneself in the matrimonial bed.

"Well mother, as you were aware I kept myself for James. Without going into too much detail, there is a side to him that I've never seen before." She leaned over towards me and smiled,

"Jane my darling, you're a young and very beautiful woman with very little knowledge of men and I know exactly where you're coming from. But you must put things into perspective and know the options you have.

"Firstly, you are now a married woman with commitments. Yes, James is his own man and I firmly believe he likes to be in control as do most men. The upside is that you live in a beautiful house with acres of land, have freedom to do your own thing, no financial worries and have staff to look after your every need. If you give James your full attention and go out of your way to please him, and I mean in all areas of the marriage, he should be proud to have you as his wife. You've only just started to experience married life and both of you have a lot of learning to do. Your father and I have had many difficulties but not as many now. What I'm about to say is for you to read between the lines. There are areas of a marriage that women sometimes have to put up with to satisfy the needs of a man; it may be far better to think of England rather than risk an ugly confrontation." She sat back into her chair and poured herself another cup of tea.

"Well thank you mother. You've touched on some good points and I will take on board what you say." She smiled and leaned forward again, "Jane my darling, I can't live your life for you. You're a strong-minded woman and only you can control your destination. I know you will give your very best in all you do but whatever road you take you know your mother will always be right beside you. Now get back off to your new home as I'm sure there are a million and one things to do." We both got up from our chairs and embraced each other.

"Thank you, mother, I love you very much." I embraced her once more then made my way back home. Whilst on my way back I kept thinking about my conversation with mother. The more I thought about it, the more it led me to believe she may have experienced a similar situation to mine, although she would never ever say. Anyway, I've decided to give my marriage a try to the best of my ability and although things have gotten off to a disappointing start, I'm quite excited to try to turn things around with James and get back the loving man I know as I want a full loving relationship and not just a married woman thinking of England.

Having arrived back home, I decided to go over to the stables to say hello to my favourite horse Marmaduke. I got him for my 21st birthday and never feel alone when I'm with him. He's such a trusted loyal companion. After getting some carrots I went across to his stable and was greeted by his usual whinny. Outside on the yard Mark, the head groom, had just come back from riding one of the other horses. As he came over towards me I couldn't help but notice the mud splatters on his knee length riding boots and jodhpurs stopping just short of the huge bulge protruding from his crotch. Although on the verge of being obscene I still wanted a quick glimpse.

"Excuse me Milady, if you're going out for a ride I will tack him up for you"

"No thank you Mark. I'll not be riding today as I have many things to attend too while my husband is away on business."

"That's fine. So, if you'll excuse me I'll carry on and get this horse cleaned out." As he turned away I saw that he also had the cutest firm backside. *I can't believe I'm having such wicked thoughts and shouldn't be looking at another man's body but what's the harm in looking? I'm sure many other women would.*

I gave Marmaduke his carrots and spent a bit of time with him before getting back to the house but before doing so I went over to Mark.

"Is everything OK in the yard and have you got all you need regarding feed etc.?"

"Yes, thank you, everything is in order and thank you for asking." As he turned and reached up for one of the hay nets, yet again I couldn't help but have another quick peep at the bulge in his pants.

"Well should you need anything please let me know because as of now I will oversee the execution of duties in the yard and ensure things are kept in good order. By the way Mark, how old are you?" He turned towards me with a concerned look on his face and said. "I'm 25 this month Milady."

"Ok that's fine, just curious and nothing to be concerned about. I'll speak to you later." I turned towards the house with a bit of a naughty smile on my face.

On entering the house, I went to see Edna the house keeper. "Is everything in order and all the laundry done and up to date? It would seem that James is a stickler for detail and everything has to be in place so I don't want him to find fault with anything upon his return."

"Yes, everything is done including all the cleaning and laundry. I've been here long enough to know that sir is very demanding regarding the upkeep of the house and everything has to be in its rightful place."

I felt relieved; she obviously knows him better than me. "Thank you, Edna. I know I can trust and depend on you, and the way you keep this house to ensure it runs like clockwork must be very challenging. It's a real credit to your enthusiasm and hard work. I most certainly won't interfere with the way you conduct your daily tasks. I'm sure you have your own lists of suppliers regarding products for the house but should you need or wish to discuss anything, please feel free to ask me."

She turned towards me with a kind smile on her face. "Thank you for those kind words as I endeavour to do my best. And yes, should I need anything I will surely see you at your convenience, thank you." With that she left and went back to her work. She is such a nice lady.

It had been a long day so I decided on an early night. I had a nice shower and retired to read my book. It would have been nice to hear from James but I guessed he must be busy with work but I'm looking forward to seeing him some time tomorrow. I just hope things will be different from now on and back to how we were before getting married. Things so far have not been very pleasant but I'm going to think positively as this is all I can do for now.

Chapter Three

It's 8 am. Time to get up, have a quick shower and then dress in something nice as James is back today and I want to give him a nice warm welcome home. Before going down for breakfast I made sure the bedroom was perfect as I didn't want to get caught by surprise with an early return. After breakfast, I went around the house for a final check, especially in the room that James had slept in but there was no need as everything was in place. Edna is really on the ball and it's such a relief to know how efficient she is. Knowing the house was in order, I made my way over to the stables to make sure the horses had been mucked out and the yard was clean. On reaching the stables I was pleased to see the horses had been turned out and everything had been done. I went to the tack room to find the stable girl cleaning and polishing the leathers. She stood up from where she was sitting and turned towards me and smiled.

"Good morning Milady,"

"Good morning. What is your name?"

"My name is Sally, Sally Goodwin."

"Well Sally, you're doing a great job. The stables and yard are as clean as a new pin. You obviously take pride in your work, very well done.

By the way is Mark in this morning? I haven't noticed him anywhere."

"Yes, he's been here since 6 am. He's just taken Duke the large cob out to give him some exercise but should be back in about half an hour."

"Ok, I'll catch up with him later in the meantime carry on with the good work." James really has a great team of staff working for him. My only concern is that he might look upon me as part of his staff too as everyone has their duty to perform. I made my way back to the house and decided to ring my best friend to see if she wanted to meet up in town one day this week. I've not seen or spoke to her since being back from Venice and it was time we caught up on all the latest gossip.

"Hi Samantha, it's Jane. How are you?"

She sounded all giggly as her usual self, "Hi Jane. We must be telepathic as I was just about to give you a call. So, tell me what's it like to be a happily married woman? Have you settled in at your new home?" *If only she knew.* "Yes, everything is good, so how about we meet up for a bit of lunch this week? I can make this Thursday if it's ok with you."

"That's fine by me. Shall we meet at our usual place in Canterbury say about 11.30 am? I'm so looking forward to seeing you and I've got lots to tell you."

"Me too, so that's a date then. I'll see you this Thursday at 11.30. You take care, bye."

I was so looking forward to seeing Samantha again we've been close friends since our early school days. She is very loyal and I can talk to her in total confidence. It was mid-afternoon and time for a coffee. I made my way to the kitchen where Edna was preparing some food.

"That smells nice Edna. What are you making?" She turned towards me, wiping her hands on her apron.

"I'm making some scones and a fruit cake as they are Master James' favourite and he will surely ask for them on his arrival back home. Have you a favourite that you would like me to bake? Only I'm at my happiest when in the kitchen baking."

"No thank you Edna, although I may have the occasional sweet thing I'm more of a savoury person. Tell me, does my husband ever get annoyed say if he wanted some cake or something similar and there wasn't any available?"

She turned towards me with a slightly concerned look on her face. "Let me just say this in confidence, as you have just got married and moved into this large house. It may take a bit of time to settle in and get to know what your husband likes and dislikes. He has very strict and set rules as to how this house should be run. If I do what is asked of me and in the exact manner he desires then he leaves me alone to carry out my duties without any confrontations, but if someone were to challenge his decisions or not do what was asked of them, then things could become very ugly and unpleasant. But I'm sure as you must know him better than most, you are already aware of this." Edna knows him and his demanding ways far better than I do and I was courting him for over two years. Never once did he show any signs of aggression or controlling behaviour.

"Yes, I must admit he does like things done in a certain way but that's just the way he is." I was saying this as if I already know and agreed with what she is saying but I was beginning to see a very dark side of the man I had just married.

"Could you tell me where you keep the coffee?" She turned towards me and smiled.

"No need. I'll make that for you, would you like it black with a jug of cream or just made with milk?" She made her way over to the cupboard and reached for the coffee.

"I'll have it black with a jug of cream please. I'll be in the drawing room."

"No problem. I will bring it in shortly."

I made my way over to the drawing room thinking that it all seemed a bit bizarre being waited on hand and foot as this was something I would normally do for myself. There was a gentle knock on the door and Edna brought in the tray with the coffee together with a plate of biscuits and placed them on the small table next to my chair.

"Thank you, Edna." She turned towards me with a kind smile.

"Is there anything else I may get you?"

"No thank you, I'll call for you should I need anything." With that she left the room. *Being waited on like this is a pleasant experience, something I can quickly get accustomed to.* I was just starting to relax when the phone rang, it was James.

"Hi James nice to hear from you darling, is everything all, right?"

"Yes, everything is fine. Now listen carefully. I will be home sooner than expected, I will arrive back at approximately 6.00 pm so will you inform the house keeper to prepare a light dinner at 7.00? I will see you soon and we can talk later."

Before I had chance to say another word he had hung up the phone. I would have thought he might at least asked how I was and if everything was ok back here. Though I was feeling quite happy just a few moments ago, I suddenly felt a bit fed up and unloved. I made my way back to the kitchen to inform Edna about tonight. She was just removing a large fruit cake from the oven.

"My husband will be back at 6.00 and has asked that you prepare a dinner for 7.00."

"That's fine. I'll make sure everything is ready and that there's enough for two."

"Thank you, Edna. I'll leave you to it." With that I left and made my way up to my room.

It was only an hour before James was due to arrive back. I best make myself look nice so I can give him a warm welcome home. After I was ready I made sure the bedroom was all neat and tidy before making my way downstairs. I went into the drawing room to take the tray back to the kitchen but Edna had already seen to it. I feel as though she's really watching my back and looking out for me. I was just about to make my way through to the lounge when the car pulled up at the front door. James was home. I don't know why but I was feeling a bit nervous as he entered the hall.

"Hello darling." I went over and kissed him on the cheek.

"Hello dear, have you informed the house

keeper regarding dinner?" I can't believe that's the first thing on his mind with no mention of asking how I am or saying how nice it is to see me.

"Yes, I told Edna as soon as you asked me. She is attending to it and dinner will be ready at 7.00 as you requested." His chauffeur brought in his overnight bag and placed it on the floor in the hall and left.

James turned towards me with what seemed to be a content look on his face. "Well everything appears to be in order. Would you take my bag to the laundry room? Then ask the housekeeper to bring some tea into the drawing room as we have to discuss how things went whilst I was away."

He then disappeared into the drawing room. I did as he asked and then spoke to Edna. "As you may have gathered my husband has just returned. Would you please make a pot of tea together with some biscuits and a portion of his favourite cake and bring it through to the drawing room?"

She turned towards me with a great big smile as I knew she had just baked it. "I'll see to it straight away it won't be long." I left her to it and went to see James.

I took a deep breath as I entered the drawing room and went over to sit in the chair opposite him.

"Well darling, it's nice to have you back. How was your business trip?"

He looked up towards me with a blank expression. "Things went better than expected hence why I'm back early. Enough about my business trip, let's get to the point. Were there any issues I should know about whilst I was away?" He's only been gone for two days, what does he think could have happened?

"As far as I'm aware everything is in order. I've spoken to Edna on several occasions to ensure she has everything she needs to carry out her duties regarding the house but she is very organised and thorough. I get on very well with her and she was always two steps ahead of me."

He looked at me in a stern manner. "I don't want you to get overly friendly with the staff, they must know their place or they will lose respect for you. They are paid and paid well to carry out their duties here." There was a gentle knock on the door and James beckoned her in, Edna wheeled in the tea trolley with the drinks and other items as required and asked if we should require anything further.

"No thank you that will be all." James replied. She nodded and left the room. I felt a bit sorry for her, she is such a nice lady and regardless what James may say I find nothing wrong in communicating with the staff in a friendly, respectful manner. I was always brought up to believe that courtesy costs nothing.

"Have you been over to the stables to check that all is in order?"

Bloody hell, it feels like I'm one of his staff and not the love of his life. "Yes, I went over yesterday and first thing this morning, mainly to see Marmaduke and give him his treat and spend a bit of time with him. But I also spoke to Mark the groom to ensure everything was in order and that all the horses were ok. You have a great team of staff as the yard and all the tack is kept in immaculate condition."

He picked up a biscuit and dunked it in his tea as he sat back in his chair, seemingly content with my answers.

"Well it would appear that you have been vigilant and that gives me peace of mind knowing that when I'm away on business you are capable of looking after my interests. Now to change the subject, Lord and Lady Benson have invited us to attend a dinner dance tomorrow evening. This is a very important event as many influential business people will be attending and it could well be very beneficial to my interests. Informing you now will ensure you have ample time to prepare whatever attire you seem fit to make me proud to have you on my arm. Now if you will excuse me I will take a shower before coming down for the evening meal."

I feel upbeat and excited at the prospect of our first time out together since being married and for such a great occasion. I'll make sure that I wear something most suitable as I really want James to feel proud of me.

Sometime later James came down wearing something casual.

"Do you feel better now that you've freshened up?"

"Yes, I do. It's near 7.00 shall we go to the dining room?" As we entered I noticed that two place settings had been neatly laid. As we sat down I just hoped that Edna would have the meal out in time. No sooner said than done the clock in the entrance hall began to chime and with impeccable timing Edna entered the room pushing a trolley containing a large selection of food. She placed the food on the dining table, including various deserts. She turned towards James and asked if he would like her to pour the wine.

"No thank you my wife and I can manage. That will be all for now." Once again, she nodded gracefully and left the room. I turned towards James and smiled, "This is very nice darling, just the two of us, Edna certainly knows how to cook and lay out a good table."

He looked over at me a bit straight faced. "As previously mentioned she is doing what she gets paid for and doesn't need complimenting every time she prepares a meal, let's not talk about staff but instead enjoy our meal together." He poured the wine and we had a most enjoyable meal and even more so because it was just the two of us.

After our meal, we retired to the lounge. I sat in a huge comfortable arm chair that was facing an open log fire. There's something magical about the smell of wood burning and watching the flames gently flicker up the chimney. I turned towards James who had just picked up a book.

"Do you love me James?" His reply was straight to the point. "I married you, didn't I? What more do you want me to say?"

He then proceeded to read his book. It wasn't the exact answer that I was hoping for but it was a start. After spending a quiet but pleasant few hours together we decided to retire. On entering the bedroom, I went to the bathroom to undress and prepare myself for bed. After the last time, we were together I was feeling a bit apprehensive not knowing what to expect. On leaving the bathroom I noticed James was already in bed.

I pulled back the sheet and slid in beside him and gently put my arm over and whispered, "James would you like to make love to me?"

He grunted a bit then mumbled, "No, I've had a long day and don't wish to be disturbed, now get to sleep."

Well that was brief, who said love was dead? "Ok I understand, good night, see you in the morning." I turned over and lay on my back, so many thoughts were going through my mind, but eventually I drifted off to sleep.

Chapter Four

I was woken up by the sound of a closing door. It seemed that James was already up and about. It's 7.30 and perhaps time to get up. I made my way to the bathroom to have a shower and noticed that James had been here before me, so I presumed he had gone downstairs. Once showered and dressed I went down stairs to find that James was in his study doing some paperwork.

"Good morning darling you're up early. Did you sleep well?"

He looked up from his desk. "Yes, I slept very well thank you just needed to finish a bit of business. As it is such a nice morning I thought we would take the horses out for a bit of exercise so I've instructed the head groom to have them tacked up and ready for 10.00. I have arranged for the housekeeper to serve breakfast at 9.00 sharp in the dining room, giving us ample time to get changed into our riding clothes and go across to the stables."

"Well what can I say? It seems you have everything arranged but yes it would be nice to go for a ride as Marmaduke hasn't been ridden for a while and he does like to be taken out." Well I must admit that took me by surprise. But hey, things do seem to be taking a turn for the better as we both used to like to go out riding out together. My fingers crossed.

So, after breakfast we got changed and went down to the stables and true to his word, both horses were tacked up and ready to go.

As we approached the horses Mark came over. "Good morning sir, good morning milady, both horses are ready as you requested." James untied and mounted his horse then instructed Mark to help me with Marmaduke, something he had always had done before but this time it seemed he was just showing off his authority. Mark released Marmaduke and clasped his hands together, offering to help me mount up, As I put my foot in his clasped hands I could feel the power and strength in his arms as he helped me up. I thanked him and then rode off with James.

We were out for about two hours before returning. We both really enjoyed it and me especially, as it felt just the same way we always were. As soon as we entered the yard both Mark and Sally came over to take control of the horses. After dismounting I wanted to thank Mark but knew James would not approve.

We left the stables and made our way back to the house and I commented to James about our ride, "I really enjoyed that darling. We must do it again soon."

"Yes, it was very relaxing but now we must concentrate on getting prepared for this very important function tonight."

Once back at the house James went into the study to make some business calls and I went up to my room. I needed to find a suitable gown to wear for this important dinner dance tonight. After much deliberation, I finally decided on my favourite powder blue gown and picked out some matching shoes. All that remained was to look through my jewellery box for a suitable necklace and matching earrings. Satisfied with my choice, I laid them out so they would be ready for tonight and then made my way back down to see James. He was still in his study.

"As we are dining out this evening, would you like me to sort out a light lunch?"

"Yes, have it made, ready in half an hour giving me time to finish this bit of paperwork." I made my way to the kitchen and on my way met Edna.

"Edna, just the person I'm looking for. We will be out this evening attending a dinner dance, therefore will not require an evening meal but what I would like for you to do is to put together some sandwiches and beverages and bring them to the drawing room in half an hour." I followed her into the kitchen.

"That is no problem I have some beautiful top side of beef."

"Yes, that sounds good I'll leave it in your very capable hands."

"Thank you, I will bring them in with the various sauces and a pot of tea to the drawing room in half an hour." Knowing Edna, you can bet it will be there on the dot and not a minute later.

On my way to the drawing room I picked up the day's newspaper, sat in my comfortable arm chair, put my feet up and enjoyed a bit of me time. Unfortunately, it was short lived, as true to form Edna arrived right on time with our lunch.

"Thank you, Edna. You can leave the trolley here." I went to the study to inform James that lunch was ready. After we had eaten James returned to his study and I got back to reading the papers. Sometime later James came into the drawing room. "Now then its 4.30, perhaps you should be thinking of preparing for tonight as we have to be leaving no later than 6.00."

"Yes, you're right James I wasn't aware of the time. I'll go up now and start getting myself ready." I hadn't realised it was so late in the afternoon.

After having a shower and drying my hair, I sat at the dressing table and began to put on my makeup. A few moments later James came in the bedroom, just as I was putting on my lipstick. He just stood there for a moment before coming across.

"Why are you wearing such a bright red lipstick? Are you trying to draw attention to yourself?" He was starting to sound quite annoyed.

"No darling not at all, I just want to look nice for you."

"Well I think you look like a bloody circus clown, in fact I'll show you." He grabbed hold of my hair and sharply pulled my head back, snatched the lipstick from my hand then drew it all over my face and neck.

"There, take a good look in the mirror. That's what a fucking clown looks like. Now get in the bathroom to get cleaned up and make yourself look like a lady and not some attention-seeking whore."

I ran crying to the bathroom and started to clean the mess off my face. I'm still finding it hard to believe this was the same man I thought I was going to love forever. Before we were married he was so kind and gentle, always holding my hand, but now he's become an abusive controlling monster. I was walking on egg shells and I feared the next time that he might strike me. I knew I had to pull myself together and avoid angering him further. I got myself cleaned up and went back to my dressing table and put on a bit of eye shadow and light make up and then carefully chose a delicate pink lipstick. A few moments later he re-entered the room and came back over. I stood up to greet him.

"Is this more of what you had in mind?"

He stood there smiling at me as I waited for his reaction. "You look absolutely stunning my dear. Now hurry along and get dressed as we must be leaving in half an hour." *Am I going bloody crazy or what, is this is a different man from 20 minutes ago,* I couldn't believe he was acting as if nothing had ever taken place. I now seriously realised that this was a very difficult and scary situation I was in and I needed time to think about how to handle it and what to do long term. That's if there's to be a long term, because now that prospect is now in serious jeopardy.

After getting dressed I put on a minimal amount of jewellery but decided against any perfume in case it may provoke a second confrontation. I joined James downstairs where the chauffeur was waiting and Edna was standing in the hall.

"You look very pretty my dear, now it's time

we were going." We went outside to the car and made our way to the venue. James turned towards me and touched my arm.

"Now as I've said before there will be a lot of influential people here tonight so you only need to speak when you are spoken to and conduct yourself in an intelligent manner. Do you understand?"

I can't believe he is saying this, I have a law degree and speak three fluent languages, I probably speak far better than him. "Yes of course darling, I will not let you down and will do as you ask." He tapped me gently on my arm in approval.

We arrived at the enormous hall and were greeted by two footmen who announced our arrival. On entering this very grand ballroom Lord and Lady Benson greeted us.

"Good evening James, so glad you to see you. Is this your beautiful wife?"

"Yes, indeed this is my adoring wife of just a few weeks."

Lord Benson turned towards me and held out his hand. "Very nice to meet you my dear now let me introduce you to Lady Benson." She stepped forward towards me; looking slightly reserved.

"Good evening my dear, you look so young and pretty and have only just married." She turned to her husband and James. "Now while you two men discuss boring business details us ladies are going to socialise with the other guests. Come along dear, I'll introduce you to some friends of mine."

After a few drinks and doing the rounds it was time to enter the dining room and be seated at our allocated seats. I sat opposite James and felt a little awkward not knowing many people around me but I felt a bit more relaxed after dinner was served as people seemed to become more talkative. The guy sitting next to me was a friend of James' who spoke out over the table to him, "I say James, how come you were you so lucky to find such a charming beautiful lady to take as your wife?" The question was a bit embarrassing but I suppose it was in good spirits.

"Well after two years of courtship I asked for her hand in marriage and to make an honest woman of her and to my delight she said yes. I simply love and adore her and couldn't imagine life without her."

"Well said that man." He then turned his attention to me. "And what say you?" I looked over at James and smiled gently.

"Yes, I feel very privileged to have met James and look forward to a very happy future together." If only they knew the truth. This was his cunning plan in leading people to believe that he is such a nice and caring man, knowing that if I said anything to the contrary they wouldn't believe me and would probably brand me a trouble-maker. After the meal, had finished Lord Benson stood up to make an announcement.

"Ladies and gentlemen, brandy is being served in the drawing room and the music is playing in the ballroom. So please make your way from the dining room and a good time will be had by all. Thank you." I left my seat and went over to James who was talking to one of his friends.

"Hello my dear. This is my friend Charles. We are just going for a brandy in the drawing room to discuss a bit of business so perhaps you should mingle with the other ladies in the ballroom and enjoy the music."

"Yes of course darling, see you soon." With that I made my way to the ball room. The sound of the music filled the room and many people were dancing. It was all very regal and the women were dressed in their lovely long gowns. I took a drink from one of the trays being brought around and stood there feeling a bit like a fish out of water until a lady who seemed to be in a similar situation came over to me.

"Hi, I don't think we've met. My name is

Georgina."

"Hi Georgina, so pleased to meet you. My name is Jane and my husband is about somewhere talking business. I was feeling a bit out of place so I very much welcome your company."

"Me too, my husband has also deserted me. They bring us out for the evening and then leave us to fend for ourselves." She was good company and we seemed to get on well. After a couple of more drinks and still no sign of our husbands, we decided to get on the dance floor and join in during some of the dances that didn't require a partner. It felt good to get in the spirit of things and I started to relax and enjoy myself as did Georgina. After two dances, we had a refill and took a seat to catch our breath. Then I saw James and his friend enter the ball room so I turned to Georgina.

"That's my husband James over there. He has just come in with one of his friends." She started to chuckle.

"What a coincidence, that friend is my husband. Come on, let's go over to them."

"Hello Charles, hello James. I was just saying how strange it was that Jane and I met each other not knowing that each of you were our husbands. I think I've found a new friend." James looked over to me and smiled.

"Well there you are my precious darling looks like you're having fun." I didn't want to sound too overly excited until Georgina chipped in. "Jane and I are having had a great time on the dance floor, are you going to have a dance with me Charles?"

"Perhaps later, now you go enjoy yourself." Then I turned to James. "Would you like to have a dance darling? They're playing some lovely music."

"Not now precious, like Charles said perhaps later." Georgina took my hand and we headed back to the dance floor.

The evening was ending and the orchestra was playing some slow romantic tunes. "James, let's have a dance together. I haven't seen much of you tonight. It would be so nice just to be close to you. Your friend and Georgina are dancing."

"Very well then, just the one." It felt good to be doing something together but it was short lived as the next dance was the "Excuse Me Waltz" and I was hoping and praying no one would come between us. We started dancing and I must admit it felt good, much like it used to be when we were courting. Then a voice said, "Excuse me" but as luck would have it was his friend Charles. He butted in to dance with me and James was dancing with Georgina and everything was fine.

Charles was a good dancer. As we were about

to go around once more, a man who was about 30 years of age and at least six-foot-six came over to excuse Charles who then swiftly met his new partner. The man looked down towards me with the most piercing blue eyes, spoke with the most gorgeous deep voice and smelt like heaven.

"Good evening, I have been waiting all night for the opportunity to have a dance with the most beautiful lady here tonight." As we danced he very gently held my hand but held my waist very firmly with the other hand. I don't know what came over me but suddenly I just went to pieces. Throughout all off my time with James or any other man, I have never experienced a feeling such as this before.

"Let me introduce myself. I'm Captain Andrew Phillips." I tried to compose myself but could only warble on like a love-sick teenager.

"Lady Jane nice to meet you Captain," he looked down and smiled, showing the most perfect set of white teeth

"Likewise, are you with someone here?" I desperately wanted to say no but had no choice.

"Yes, I'm with my husband who is on the dance floor nearby," *and I'm sure he will be watching me*, I Knew that I had best be very lady like and emphasize the fact that I have no control over the dance, as it's up to the males to change partners.

"I've just got to say that he is a very lucky man and I am truly envious of him." Just then another man came over and asked me to dance. Due to the nature of the dance I assumed I was about to change partners but Captain Phillips turned towards him and said, "Sorry my good man but I have only just had the pleasure so perhaps another time." He was just so masterful and taking his size into account I don't think many would dare challenge him. As we were dancing near I was aware of his manliness occasionally touching me, sending a strange sensation through my entire body. Then all too soon the music stopped.

"Thank you, Lady Jane, it has been a great pleasure to have made your acquaintance," With that he left and I made my way off the dance floor and over to James. As the evening ended the guests began to leave and we were bid goodnight by the hosts Lord and Lady Benson. On our way, back to the car I held James' hand.

"Thank you for a lovely evening plus I've made a new friend with Georgina."

"Yes, it was most enjoyable and you looked very radiant my dear." I wasn't sure if this was a genuine compliment or if it was leading up to something more sinister.

Chapter Five

The car pulled up the drive to the front entrance. The chauffeur came around to open the rear doors and escorted us in to the house.

"Will that be all Sir?"

"Yes, but be sure to have the car around at 9.00 in the morning as I have an important business meeting to attend." The chauffeur acknowledged his request and left.

It was very late and we retired to bed. No sooner had we entered the bedroom James came over and grabbed my arm. "So, who was that man you were dancing with?" As he looked at me with those menacing eyes I thought, *oh shit, something bad is about to happen.* I tried to shrug it off as though it meant nothing.

"I don't know who he was darling, I was dancing with your friend Charles when he just appeared, and as it was an Excuse Me dance I didn't really have any choice. He stepped in and Charles moved on to the next dancer. He was a bit clumsy and awkward not as light on his feet as you."

I could tell he wasn't convinced. "I saw the way you looked up at him gazing into his eyes, I'm not stupid."

"I had no choice but to look up to him as he was so incredibly tall and the only words we spoke were just thank you at the end of the dance.

"I don't believe it you were both having a conversation and smiling at each other. The truth is you probably fancied him." *To bloody right I did.* I tried to stay calm as I could see he was becoming very angry.

"Darling please, you're seriously imagining something that just never happened. It was just a dance, so let's get ready for bed as I'm really exhausted." He turned me around and then forcefully pushed me over the edge of the bed.

"So, I'm imagining things am I? Well imagine this bitch." He pulled up my gown and ripped off my underwear leaving me exposed from the waist down. Next thing I felt was a searing pain across my buttocks as he began to thrash me with what felt like a belt strap. I cried out,

"Please James, please stop. Don't do this to me; I haven't done anything wrong."

"Well perhaps this will be a reminder for the future as not to show me up again." Before I realised what was happening his erection penetrated me, fucking me as hard as he could, but the pain from my buttocks was far greater than this pain. Thankfully it quickly finished with him relieving himself inside me.

"There bitch, that's no more than you deserved. Now get to the bathroom and out of my sight." Feeling dejected I went to the bathroom and had a shower as I just felt so dirty. Looking in the mirror, I could see the welt marks on my buttocks from where he'd hit me. Throughout the entire evening, I conducted myself in a most proper manner, speaking only to other ladies and at no time did I give James cause to react in the way he did. After putting on my nightwear I went over to the bed only to find him out cold and snoring. Pulling back the sheets, I gently got into bed so as not to disturb him but bearing in mind of how much he had to drink it was highly improbable. With my buttocks still burning, I tried to get some sleep. On reflection, having danced with the very tall and most handsome Captain Phillips, I told myself it was well worth the pain. So, he didn't win after all.

Six Months Later

It was 6.00 in the morning and I was wide awake as I didn't sleep well, hardly surprising after yet another painful ordeal last night. Since it was such a grand morning with the sun just rising, I decided to get up and go to the stables to spend some time with Marmaduke as he is always pleased to see me. As I made my way over to the stables everything was quiet apart from the dawn chorus and on the lake, were two swans showing perfect reflections, while the sun danced on the still water. It just felt so nice and peaceful but as I walked past the hay loft I thought I heard voices coming from within. Feeling curious and somewhat nervous I quietly tip toed into the tack room that was adjoined to the hay loft and peered through the small gap between the door and frame.

I gasped in astonishment. It was Mark and the stable girl kissing and removing each other's clothing. I should have barged in right there and then and put a stop to it and had the two of them instantly dismissed but curiosity got the better of me because as wrong as it was, I wanted to see more. He laid a rug down over two bales of hay and sat her down, as he stood in front of her she started to undo his belt. I was reminded of the day when I was here at the stables and couldn't help but notice the huge bulge in his tight riding pants. I was excited then but now as I was about to see exactly what he's got. Quiet as a mouse I waited and watched as she pulled down his britches and then with both hands slid down his tight boxer shorts, exposing the biggest shaft imaginable. It must have been at least 9 inches long with an incredible girth.

She held it with both hands and gently rubbed it up and down while stroking his tight balls, then moving her head forward her tongue started to lick and tease the tip of the shiny head before engulfing it into her wide-open mouth. With long gentle strokes, she began moving her head up and down on his now well lubricated shaft while at the same time stroking his hairy sack. Having achieved a full erection, he stepped back and then removed her bra exposing her large firm breasts which he kissed passionately before laying her down on the rug. She raised her buttocks as he slid down her panties revealing her dark hairy sex. He knelt between her thighs as she placed her legs over each of his shoulders then with each hand placed firmly under her buttocks he began to pleasure her with his tongue. I should have felt disgusted as what I was seeing but quite the contrary, having no sexual experience I was intrigued and must confess that right then I was feeling so fucking horny and in such a high state of sexual arousal, unlike anything I've ever felt before.

A few moments later Mark stood up showing his huge erection. After parting her thighs, he bent down towards her. She cried out as he penetrated her eagerly awaiting sex with that beautiful erect shaft. By this time feeling how wet I'd become, I couldn't help but touch myself wishing it was me in there instead of her. They fucked each other for what must have been ten minutes before climaxing and both looked exhausted. Time for me to leave. After what I had just witnessed it was hard to believe how bloody green and inexperienced I was. At this moment, I was feeling so down and lonely in desperate in need of affection. I wanted to be made love to in a romantic and caring way, to receive and give oral sex to a man, but the stark reality is that I will never experience such things being the way they are. James just uses me purely for his own selfish gratification, to relieve himself where and when it suits him with no intention of making me feel like a loved woman. But believe me, after what I have just witnessed things must change, and in the very near future.

When I got back to the house James was in the drawing room, I tried to act calm and normal but it was difficult after what I had just seen.

"Hi darling, where have you been?" There he goes again as if everything was just dandy.

"I went over to the stables to spend a bit of time with Marmaduke."

"Good, I wondered where you were. As it's such a grand morning why don't you take him out?" *If only he really knew what I was doing and what's more what I really wanted*, He could certainly learn a lot from Mark about how to make love and please a woman.

"No not today as I've arranged to see my friend Samantha in Canterbury at 11.00. We're meeting for a coffee and to do a spot of shopping."

"Jolly good, you go and enjoy yourself. Now I must get ready as I must leave at 9.00 sharp to attend a business meeting. I might not be back till late so don't wait up." He came over and kissed me on the cheek before disappearing.

I had a light breakfast before getting ready to see my friend but all the time was thinking about recent events, I certainly felt envious of them and kept wishing it had ben me in that hay loft. It was time to go. I got my coat and bag and set off to Canterbury. After parking the car I made my way to the coffee shop where Samantha was already waiting. She stood up to greet me and after a big hug we ordered some drinks and treated ourselves to a slice of cake. I took off my coat and placed it on the back of the chair.

"Well Jane my darling you're looking very well it would seem married life suits you. So, come on and tell me all about it." I know she's my best friend but I dared not tell all as some things must stay private. Plus, she might think I'm partially to blame.

"Well things are OK. James seems to have changed a bit and spends a bit of time away on business but that is something I guess I'll have to get used to."

She started laughing and leaned towards me speaking in a soft tone, "Welcome to the club. Men can be such bastards at times. But take it from me my dear Jane, let them think they're in control and then do what you want when they're away on these so-called business trips, because believe you me they will be shagging around and don't be fooled in to believing anything different. I know you think that James wouldn't do that to you but it won't be long before you see the tell-tale signs. Men are easily tempted, but as the saying goes 'While the cats away the mice will play.'"

"I can't believe you Samantha, whatever next," I said and started giggling.

"I've been married 10 years and I know John has had other women while away on business. I just accept it let them think you're the innocent faithful wife at home while they're getting away with it. In the meantime, oblivious to them you're busy doing your own thing and everyone is happy. Just be discrete if you decide to treat yourself to another slice of cake." We both started laughing.

"Well I must admit there are times when another slice of cake would go down well."

"Welcome to the club, now let's get out of here

and do the shops." I felt so relieved talking to Samantha as it would appear I'm not the only woman with problems. I didn't mention anything about what I saw this morning as that was my little secret.

After a few hours shopping and another drink, we made our way back home. I was starting to feel good about myself again as I've really tried with James in that department but now realise that if things don't change soon then what Samantha suggested may be something to consider.

Chapter Six

On arriving back home Edna approached me from the kitchen. "Would you wish for an evening meal?"

"Perhaps not a meal as I've had a substantial lunch today while out with a friend. But latcr say about 6.00, a bowl of soup and a roll would be nice."

"No problem I'll have it ready. Where would you like me to bring it?"

"I'll have it in the lounge please."

"Very well, in the meantime is there anything else I may get you?"

"No thank you Edna." With a nod of the head she smiled then made her way back towards the kitchen. In the meantime, I decided to run a nice hot bath, change into something more comfortable and just have a nice relaxing evening all to myself in front of the lovely log fire. Then like clockwork Edna brought in the meal trolley with soup, rolls and an assortment of cake and biscuits plus a pot of tea.

"Edna that looks really nice." She placed the trolley to the side of me and asked if that would be all. "Yes, thank you, I will see you in the morning."

After a bite to eat I put my feet up and settled down with my book. Even though it was a very good read my mind kept getting distracted by what I saw this morning across at the stables. As much as I tried to and clear it from my mind, the desire to be made love to was over whelming, I desperately needed to feel loved and wanted

No news from James so I expect he will be back late but I thought he would have at least rang me even if it's just to say hello. I was confounded trying to understand the fact that he firmly believed I was his personal property to control and use in any way he deemed fit. The fact that he openly portrayed himself as the perfect gentleman and devoted husband while in other people's company would make it extremely difficult for anyone to think otherwise

It was getting late so I retired to my room and went to bed. I was not in the mood for reading as there was too much going on in my head. I must have dozed off as the sound of the bedroom door opening woke me. It was James and he quietly got undressed and slid into bed. I pretended to be asleep but within a few seconds of him beside me I detected the strong smell of perfume, something we women are very good at. Samantha was right, men can be such bastards even more so considering the short time we had been married. It would be futile to challenge him as I know he would outright deny any wrong doing and get very annoyed at the prospect of being challenged to say the least.

Thinking of what my good friend Samantha said, I realized I had the choice of being treated as a door mat for the rest of my life and living like a hermit, or I could have a change of strategy and let him think he's getting away with having me as his timid, happy, unsuspecting wife, while I'm out enjoying life in the manner I choose. The alternative of leaving him at this moment in time is not a sensible option, as he says should I ever leave him, he will always find me and to "expect extreme consequences." Most people except for my friend Samantha would seriously doubt that he could ever do anything terrible and would probably side up with him, especially my father who thinks the sun shines out of his you know where.

So, I decided to temporarily play the role of the devoted wife. When he's away on his business trips I will make sure the house and stables are in order then I'll take time out to pursue other interests.

After a light sleep, I checked the time. It was 6.30. I went to the bathroom and on my way back to bed I thought I would test the water and initiate the first move to see what his reaction would be. After sliding in between, the sheets and positioning myself I slowly moved my hand across his thighs but just as I touched him he grabbed my hand.

"What the fuck do you think you're playing at woman?" It wasn't the reaction I was expecting as he firmly pushed my hand away.

"I thought you would be pleased that I was feeling sexy and take the initiative." He sat up and seemed unimpressed with my gesture.

"I decide when we have sex like I decide and have the final say on everything else around here and the sooner you get it through that thick skull of yours the better for all concerned." With that I got out of bed and went into the bathroom to get dressed. After that little episode of rejection my strategy for the near future in the relationship was firmly embedded. Apart from being controlling, I wondered if the other reason for his frustration may be sexual in that he is unable to perform or keep an erection for probably more than a minute. At least not with me.

Knowing I was a virgin with no experience in that area, he seems to believe I would never question anything he does, perhaps that may have been the case. But now having seen two people share an intimate and physical embrace of making love, it's an experience I truly desire and crave for.

Chapter Seven

As I emerged from the bathroom, James came over and kissed me on the cheek.

"Sorry I got cross darling, it's just that I've got a lot of business things on my mind. Now when you're ready I'll see you down for breakfast and afterwards we can go for a ride. I'll instruct the groom to get the horses tacked up." He left the room and made his way downstairs. *He seriously thinks that his saying sorry and a kiss on the cheek makes everything ok?* Well it fucking well doesn't. As much as I love Marmaduke I really didn't feel in the mood for riding but I decided to pretend that I was, because right now I just couldn't face another confrontation.

So, after breakfast we went to the stables where both horses were tacked up and waiting, and as usual Marmaduke greeted me as I went up to him and gave him a carrot. Mark came over and helped me mount while the stable girl held the reigns. I looked at her with envy. *Your lucky bitch.* I wondered if they would be at it again whilst we were out riding. Although I wasn't in the mood for riding, I must admit it was nice to have a bit of time out with Marmaduke as he really enjoys going out for some exercise. After a couple of hours out we returned to the yard and after leaving the grooms to attend to the horses we went back to the house. On the way, back James informed me that after the weekend he would be away for the week on business and to make sure everything here on the estate was running properly. Since he only just mentioned it, I was very curious about his business trip.

"Where will you be going darling?" I was trying to sound interested and not just nosey.

"Well since you ask I have businesses to attend in France and Belgium but in the future my dear, please do not question or interfere in my business activities." I couldn't really care less where he goes, I was just playing the good wife game and couldn't wait until he was gone. It had been a bit of a long weekend stuck in the house with James, as being so possessive he disliked me to go out whilst he's at home even with my best friend. So, to keep the peace I did as he asked and pretended to pamper him and to enjoy the usual ritual of him using my body.

It was 8.00am and James was about to leave as the chauffeur puts his case in the car.

"Well it's time I was leaving, now make sure you keep an eye on things here and I'll see you on my return late Friday afternoon." He gave me a peck on the cheek.

"Now you be careful darling. I hope everything goes well and you come back safely." With that he got in the car and disappeared down the drive. If I do say so myself I think that was a convincing send off by the caring obedient wife.

Yes, yes, yes, I was free for a whole week, how exciting. Before going back in the house, I went across to the stables as I just felt in the mood to take out my favourite horse for a gallop and feel the wind in my hair. Mark was on the yard fixing a new bolt on one of the stable doors.

"Good morning Milady. Is there something I can do for you?" As he stood up, his britches again were straining to contain the bulge in his pants. *Got to stop looking at it.*

"Yes, would you prepare my horse and have him ready to go in an hour's time? By the way there's no sign of Sally, is she not in today?"

"No Milady she has taken a week's leave due to her to visiting friends in her home town in Ireland."

Just then I just had a very wicked thought. *Well I am in charge.* "Instead of just mine Mark, you can saddle up two horses, one of your choice but not my husband's. You will then accompany me on a hack just in case of any misfortune."

He looked somewhat bewildered at my unsuspecting request.

"Very well Milady, I'll see to it right now. They will be ready as you requested in an hour." With a smile on my face I made my way back to the house to get changed into my riding gear. Before returning to the stables I informed Edna that I was going out for a ride but neglected to mention that Mark was to accompany me. This was to cover my back in case for any reason James might ring and enquire as to my whereabouts.

As I entered the yard both horses were tacked up and tied to the railings. Mark appeared and looked very smart, having changed his riding britches.

"Are we all set to go?"

He walked over towards me. "Yes, Milady would you permit me to help you mount?" *It's him I'd like to mount.* I couldn't believe I was having such thoughts. I had this overwhelming and I think perfectly natural desire to be fucked by a real man. After all, in all honesty what woman doesn't?

"Yes, if you would be so kind." He came around, cupped his hands, and firmly gave me a lift and then passed me the reins. After easily mounting his horse we left the yard and headed towards the open fields. After a few minutes of riding we broke into a canter and in the distance, I saw the beginning of the woods. I turned towards Mark and with a smile on my face I yelled,

"Come on, I'll race you to the edge of the woods." He started laughing as we set off at a full gallop. At first I was in front but Mark, being the more experienced rider was soon alongside me. As he galloped past me the sight of his small but firm backside sent my heart and hormones racing faster than these two horses could ever go. It just felt like I was single and back in my teens. This was something I once felt with James and used to do but sadly feel no more, as he has changed beyond recognition.

After a most enjoyable ride we returned to the yard. Mark dismounted then came over and held Marmaduke while I did the same.

"Thank you Mark you're a very competent rider and the horses have had a really good work out. I'll leave them in your capable hands so you can put them into their stables."

"Very well Milady and may I be so bold as to say that you too are an excellent rider."

"Well thank you, now I really must take my leave." I made my way back to the house where

Edna was in the hall cleaning the large oval mirror. She turned her attention towards me,

"Have you had a pleasant ride Milady?"

"Yes, it was nice to be out in the open air. Would you prepare some lunch in half an hour? All that fresh air has given me quiet an appetite I'll take it in the drawing room."

Before having lunch, I went to my room to have a shower and a change of clothes. Having freshened up I made my way back downstairs where Edna was waiting to advise me that I had a phone call from my friend Samantha whilst I was in the shower.

"Thank you, Edna, I'll see to it right now." I went to the drawing room and made the return call.

"Hi Samantha, sorry I missed you I was in the shower. How are you?"

"I'm very well and all is good with the world how about you?"

"Me too, James is away for the week and I've just got back from my ride and I asked the groom to take one of the other horses out with me." I spoke in a soft tone and looked around making sure no one was eavesdropping.

"Tell me Jane was this groom male or female?" I could hear her giggling.

"Never mind that, did you want to meet up for lunch? I'm free all this week."

"Yes, that's why I rang because Jeff is away as well and I thought perhaps Wednesday might be a good day and you can tell me all about your ride out with the groom." She really is a big tease.

"Wednesday will be fine, I'll meet you at our usual place at 10.00 and all will be revealed." Knowing Samantha her week will be far from boring.

"That's great. I'll look forward to that, see you soon. Bye." I don't like saying too much on the phone as you can never be sure you're not being overheard.

After lunch, I drove down to the local village to get a few things and on my return made a small detour and called in at my mother's.

"Hello mother, are you well? I've just called at the village for a bit of shopping."

"I'm fine dear, get sat down and I'll make some tea. How's that husband of yours? I've not seen him for ages. Are you both beginning to settle down to married life now?" If only she really knew but it wouldn't be fair to burden her with what I'm going through.

"James is away all this week abroad on

business. I try to take an interest in what he does but just hit a brick wall and I am told it's not my concern."

"Well I expect he has a lot on his plate and doesn't want you to worry. Your father was a bit like that so in the end I never used to bother. I still don't see that much of him since his retirement as he spends most of his time down at the golf club where it's male only membership."

"Well it all seems a bit strange. I used to see more of James before we got married but now it's far less as he spends so much time away on business."

She turned towards me and smiled. "I know exactly how you feel but in time you get used to it and start to enjoy your own company and get involved in other interests. In fact, I look forward to him going to the golf club, it leaves me to enjoy my day and not have to constantly run around after him. When he's at home he's always getting under my feet." It seemed she had been in a similar situation as me perhaps not so much in the physical torment area but even if that were the case my mother would never say and I would certainly never tell her about James. One thing I did know is I was not prepared to spend the rest of my life in a loveless relationship and to be controlled in such an abusive manner. Even through him being so abusive I have really tried my best to be a loving caring wife but sadly to no avail.

"Well perhaps you're right. It's early days yet and only time will tell." We had our tea and a nice hour together then had a hug before I set off back home. Having arrived back I went through to the lounge and stretched out on the settee in front of the fire. No sooner had I gotten comfortable there was a knock on the door. It was Edna.

"Excuse me Milady, I have some errands to attend to in the morning and will not be back until lunch time, is there anything I can get you now?"

"No thank you Edna and I'll not be requiring breakfast in the morning." She acknowledged me and left the room. With the chauffeur, away, James away and Edna away until lunch time I had the house to myself. My mother was right sometimes it is nice to be on your own. I was just starting to feel a bit tired now so time for bed and a read before going to sleep, as per usual no phone call from James to see if I'm all right or to say "I love and miss you." Hard to believe he's such an uncaring bastard.

After a good night's sleep I woke up with the sun just rising over the horizon. It had just turned 5.30 and being such a grand morning I decided to get dressed and make my way over to the stables and see my lovely horse. He's such a trusted loyal companion. On my way, over to the stables it felt so nice and peaceful with only the sound of the birds breaking the silence and as I approached the yard a light was shining through the partly open door of the tack room. Cautiously I went closer but there was no need for concern as it was Mark the groom working on one of the bridles.

"Good morning Mark, you're up early." He turned towards me with a startled look on his face as I must have caught him unaware.

"Good morning Milady, I'm just putting a new buckle on this harness. I always start at 6.00 to turn the horses out so they can enjoy a full day in the field leaving me ample time to do the yard and tend to things like this holster. Will you be riding today?"

"No, I've just come to see Marmaduke and give him a treat and to enjoy the early morning sun." As he stood there repairing the bridle my eyes once again latched on to the bulge within his tight pants. What made it more exciting was I knew how big it really was and my mind was now having seriously naughty thoughts that could land me in deep, deep trouble. But the rush of adrenaline began taking over as my body was starting to feel both nervous and excited. It's 6am and there's only the two of us, so fuck it, now's the time to make my move.

"Is there plenty of hay? Only I was recently made aware that good quality hay could be in short supply this year. He put down his tools and turned towards me. "What we have in stock was only delivered last week and is top quality meadow hay of mixed grasses from last season. It is stacked separately to the rear of the loft and will only be used when the existing stock is gone. Keeping it on a continuous rotation ensures the hay remains of good quality and I know exactly where each batch that's been delivered came from."

Well he certainly has things in order, I'm really impressed. "I would like to see the last delivery if would you show me where it is?" I followed him through into the barn.

"It's all up their Milady and the hay down here is what we're using now. The stairs are very secure as is the hand rail should you wish to inspect it." I walked up close to him and smiled as I knew he had no idea what was coming next.

"Mark, are you seeing anyone or in a relationship?" He looked at me in a bewildered way, not sure on how to answer. "No Milady not at this very moment, may I ask the reason?"

"Just curious Mark that's all, now you go on up first and I will follow." As he made his way up the stairs I quickly and quietly secured the barn door before following him up.

"Well this is it and I think you will agree Milady it's of top quality."

Feeling somewhat apprehensive I went up close to him, considered his gorgeous blue eyes and whispered in a soft tone, "Mark, there was never any concern about the quality of the hay but what I'm about to say is going to be strictly just between the two of us and under no circumstance will you ever discuss or reveal this to any one as the consequences would be so severe, do you understand?"

He looked very anxious and understandably totally confused. "Of course, Milady, I would never betray your trust and you can rest assured of my total loyalty to you but what might it be that you request of me?"

Still looking him in the eye I began to speak in a whisper, "At this very moment you're going to see me not as your boss but as a woman you're about to be intimate with, yes that's right Mark. I want you to make love me. There are no strings attached and no conditions, it is purely for sexual gratification. So, do you find me desirable?"

He nervously replied, "Absolutely Milady, as would any man, you are indeed a very beautiful woman". Having recently felt so down and lonely, hearing those words help retrieve my confidence and self-esteem. I gently pressed my lips on his and once realising this was for real he started to respond by gently kissing my top lip until our tongues were exploring each other's mouths. After an amazing full on kiss the like I've not ever had before, I could feel his erection grow and press against my groin.

He stood back half a step and looked me in the eye as he started to unbutton my dress. After removing it from my arms it slid gently to the floor leaving me in just my bra and panties. As I stepped out of my dress he picked it up and carefully laid it out on top of one of the hay bales, then reached out his hand for me to sit down. Then he skilfully with one hand unfastened my bra exposing my bare breasts.

He removed his shirt displaying an amazing six pack with each muscle casting a shadow over the next. From placing his shirt next to my dress, he turned towards me standing within just a few inches of my face. I had never been in this situation with a man before but instinct took over. I removed his belt buckle and pulled down the zip of his tight britches and with a hand on either side gently pulled them down leaving just his boxer shorts.

As I raised my hands and pulled them down I gasped in disbelief at the size of this beautiful penis that gave off a light musky aroma. I knew what he wanted as did I but it was something I had never even tried or done before. Nervously I put my hand around its thick girth and began to rub it up and down and within seconds could feel him swell to a full erection. If I'm ever to become an experienced woman I've got to go the whole way. I leaned forward to the hard-shiny head and after teasing it with my tongue somehow gently eased it in my mouth and began to work on it. He gave out a moan of pleasure as he put his hands on the back of my neck and began gentle simulated thrusts in rhythm with my mouth. It was a strange but very sensual and satisfying experience knowing I was pleasing a man in this way.

A few moments later he gently pulled away, then lay me down full length on the bale of hay and began kissing my neck then down to my breasts, teasing my already hard nipples. Just as I thought things couldn't feel any better he went down kissing past my waist line, then with one hand on either side of my waist removed my silk panties. At this moment, I thought he was going to penetrate me but instead introduced me to a world of sexual bliss I never knew existed. With his head now between my thighs, he pressed his lips firmly onto my soft mound and began to pleasure me with his tongue, I placed my hands around the back of his head wanting him to take me all the way. This was my first ever experience of receiving oral sex, an experience not to be missed sending every nerve end tingling with desire. Sensing my high state of arousal, Mark slowly moved up my body while continually kissing me, on reaching my breasts I felt the head of his erection seek my eagerly awaiting opening, eagerly I pulled down on him as he reached full penetration, sending me towards the end of my ultimate desire.

He began to fuck me in a perfect rhythm while at the same time with an exacting pressure began to massage my already hard and sensitive nipples. With this combination of uncontrollable emotion I was about to experience something truly wonderful. Crying out, I grabbed his arms sinking my nails deep into his firm flesh as my entire body exploded into an uncontrollable orgasm. Throughout the entire experience, he kept moving very slowly inside me, taking me all the way until I was completely exhausted. With a slight change of pace, I felt his body go rigid as with one final thrust came deep inside me.

I wanted him to stay there a bit longer, but perhaps feeling a bit awkward he gently pulled out. I sat up as he began to get dressed but still couldn't help but notice once again that beautiful shaft that had just given me so much pleasure and of course the man behind it. He certainly knows what buttons to press to please and satisfy a woman. I'm not ashamed to admit that perhaps like most women I have pleasured myself to an orgasm. But never in my wildest dreams could I have ever imagined the intensity and beauty of an orgasm that was created by the skill and touch of an experienced and caring lover. Such a magical and memorable experience.

"Thank you, Mark, that was very touching. Now please take your leave; I will join you shortly as soon as I have re-arranged my clothing." He turned towards me and nodded as he made his exit.

Feeling a bit vulnerable on my own and still completely naked, I quickly got dressed and made my way down and back to the tack room. Mark was already back working on the same bridle as if nothing had taken place. I went over to him and whispered in his ear,

"You're a fantastic lover but just remember what was said; it's our little secret."

"Yes Milady, absolutely," I gave him a peck on the cheek and made my way back to the house thinking. *What the fuck have I just done?* I must have been totally and completely out of my tiny brainless mind, but on second thoughts, the fulfilment I have just experienced combined with the glowing feeling of being desired, something as a woman I was so desperately missing, far outweighed the risk. Yes, I am aware of the saying "Two wrongs don't make a right", but why should I feel so guilty knowing that bastard's been doing it all along?

Hindsight is a marvellous thing, but if I knew that with the right person sex could be so beautiful, I would probably have lost my virginity some time back. Had I been experienced in these matters before meeting James, I would certainly not have succumbed to his unruly behaviour towards me and most certainly wouldn't have taken his hand in marriage, but being a virgin I always believed that saving one's self for the right man was how it was meant to be. I always envisaged sex would be something beautiful between two people but after experiencing sex for the first time with James, it was at the very least disappointing, quite demoralising, and yes bloody painful. I had never been in a physical relationship before so had nothing to compare it to. It was only by chance when I saw Mark and that girl having sex in the barn that I realised just how very sensual and beautiful it could be. It's what I also desired, to feel like a woman while being made love to; not to have my body continuously used like a piece of meat for his brutal two minutes of gratification.

Once back in the house I went to my room and had a much-needed shower. I couldn't believe how good I felt about myself, especially having regained my confidence and self-esteem; I felt like a real woman. No more would I let James intimidate me, but I would still have to do my best not to cause a confrontation. I now knew for sure that he firmly believed I would accept his abuse as being normal and out of my control, since believing he was the only man I had ever slept with. How fucking wrong was he now? The only consolation was that when he does do it, the horror only lasts two minutes and it allows him to continue thinking that he's the world's greatest lover. Next time he uses my body I will no doubt want to say *"Someone has been there before you and done it properly, you fucking loser"*. Even though I can't, I'll still have the gratification of knowing.

I felt so happy I started singing on my way down stairs and into the drawing room where Edna was polishing the coffee table,

"Hello Milady, you're in fine spirits this morning and very nice to hear so,"

"Yes Edna, it's such a lovely day, one can't help but be happy. Don't you agree?"

She stood up and smiled "Absolutely Milady, I've not long been back from attending my errands and was about to ask if you would like me to prepare lunch."

"Yes, please that would be great as I do have a bit of an appetite. I'll have it here in the drawing room."

"I'll attend to it right away, it will be ready and with you in half an hour." She picked up the polish box and made her way into the kitchen.

A car caught my eye as it came up the drive towards the house. I wasn't expecting visitors and it wasn't my parents. I went to the door, intrigued as to who it might be. It was Gordon, a close friend of James who was also his accountant.

"Hello Gordon what brings you out here on this fine sunny day?"

"Hello Jane, so nice to see you." He came over and gave me a kiss on the cheek.

"I've brought some papers over for James to sign."

"Well he's away on business and not expected back until Friday but you're more than welcome to leave them in his office and I'll tell him you called as soon as he arrives back."

He looked towards me and smiled. "Yes, I know James is away but since I happened to be nearby so I took the opportunity and called in on the off chance that perhaps someone might be in. I hope I'm not being intrusive."

"Not at all, please come on in." He picked up his briefcase and entered the hall.

"Can I get you a drink of tea or coffee? I'm about to have one."

"Well I'm on a bit of a tight schedule but why not? Yes, I'd love a coffee."

"Splendid. If you'd like to take a seat in the drawing room here I'll just nip to the kitchen and advise the house keeper." I asked Edna to make coffee for two and delay lunch for 30 minutes then made my way back to the drawing room to join Gordon.

"Coffee won't be long. So, how's business with you? Are you keeping busy?"

"Yes, very much so, anyway enough talk about work; How's life treating you? I haven't seen or spoken to you since you got married."

"Life's very good thank you. I'm really enjoying the challenge of helping to run the estate." He looked up at me with that cheeky mischievous grin of his.

"Well something must be doing you good as you look absolutely marvellous." I know what he's insinuating and it's true but not with the man he believes it to be.

"Yes, I must admit I'm so happy and content

being married to James and so miss him when he's away." I must be careful as to what I say as he and James are very close. There was a knock on the door. It was Edna bringing in the coffee.

"Thank you, Edna, that will be all." She put down the tray and left.

"How's your wife Gordon? I very rarely have contact with her. Is she well?" He took a sip of his drink. "Yes, she's fine thank you, sometime soon when James is back we'll all have to meet up and go for an evening meal."

I couldn't think of anything worse, "That would nice, something I shall look forward to."

He finished his drink and placed the cup on the tray. "Well Jane, time I was making tracks. It's been so nice to see you and thanks for the coffee but before I forget here are those papers for James." He opened his briefcase and handed me a thick brown sealed envelope.

"Thank you, I'll put them on his desk in a moment." I then escorted him to the front door.

"Once again thank you for coffee and I'll speak with James on arranging that evening out." He came over and kissed me on the cheek before getting in his car then waved as he drove off. He was just a bit too familiar for my liking. As soon as he had gone

Edna came from within the kitchen.

"Would you like your lunch now Milady? It's all ready."

"Yes, please Edna. I'll take it in the drawing room and would you bring a bottle of red wine please?" She acknowledged me with a nod and went back to the kitchen.

After a late lunch, I picked up the papers and went to the lounge for a quiet read and relax in my favourite arm chair. It was no use, as much as I tried it was impossible to concentrate. All I could think about was the amazing sex that I had just had with Mark. I hoped it was good for him too and that he hadn't noticed or realized that I was so inexperienced.

Chapter Eight

It was Wednesday morning. I was up, showered, dressed and off to meet up with my best friend Samantha. I parked up and went into the coffee bar where she was already waiting for me.

"Hi Samantha, I thought being a bit early I would be here before you but you beat me to it."

She looked over and smiled. "Yes, I was a bit early, the reason being I dropped off my mother to visit her sister who lives nearby and said I would pick her up later my way back. Anyway, how are things with you? You're looking very radiant, is married life on the way up?" If only she knew but I daren't tell. This was something I had to keep a tightly guarded secret.

"Well perhaps it is because James is away all week and I'm all on my own to do whatever I please like coming out for a coffee morning with you."

She started chuckling and had that mischievous look in her eye. "Or would it possibly have something to do with riding out in the country side again with that handsome groom?"

I don't know if it was guilt but I became all hot and dithered. "Not at all, now let's order some coffee and a bit of lunch." We got our order and sat at a table in the corner by the window. Samantha couldn't wait for a bit of gossip.

"Jane you're blushing and you've gone bright red, so what's this about you and your groom going for a ride out together? Have you got a crush on him or perhaps another ulterior motive?"

I couldn't help but giggle. "You've got a one-track mind and it was nothing of the sort. He was just about to take one of the other horses out for some exercise and I just suggested we could ride out together and that's all there was to it."

"Ok then but would you have ridden out together if James was at home?"

"Well perhaps not but it's not much fun riding out on your own so I thought it would be nice to have a bit of company as he was going out anyway."

She wasn't going to leave it there. She leaned over and spoke in a bit of a whisper, "Tell me about this groom, is he young and fit?"

It was no good, she's not going to let up until I tell her something so I leaned back over and spoke in a soft tone, "Well if you must know he's 25, about 6'2", very fit and his britches are straining to keep this huge bulge contained between his thighs, so now what do you think?"

"I think you're one very lucky bitch; I'm feeling horny just thinking about him, so when can I come over and see this stud?" A couple at the next table looked across as we both started laughing aloud.

"You're not going to. He's all mine and not for sharing. Now let's talk about something else." We had a good chat and caught up on all the gossip and did a bit of shopping before she had to leave and pick up her mother.

Samantha is a good friend and I know whatever we say to each other stays just between us. But I still wouldn't indulge the fact that I fucked Mark as I think that would be tempting fate.

I arrived back home at 3.00 and as it was still such a nice sunny day I decided to go for a walk around the gardens and pick a few flowers for the house. The kitchen garden was completely surrounded by a 10' high brick wall that had grape vines and trained fruit trees attached to it. The main garden was filled with perfectly straight rows of various vegetables and flowers with everything in immaculate order and not a weed in sight. I made my way to the sheds at the far end of the garden hoping to find George the gardener and ask about what flowers I could pick for the house. George I would say is about 55years in age, stocky build and completely bald but it suits his masculine character. The first door that I entered was full of tools and mowers but I could hear someone in the adjoining shed. As I entered George was breaking up some old pots on the bench.

"Hi George are you having a bad day?"

He turned around and chuckled. "No Milady, I'm just breaking up some old damaged pots to use as crock for in the bottom of those pots over there before filling them with compost, it ensures good drainage and is far better than using gravel plus it puts these old broken pots to good use."

"Well you learn something every day. But I must say George the gardens are a true credit to you and something you're obviously very passionate about. The reason I wanted to find you is that I was looking for some suitable flowers to pick for the house and hoped you could advise me."

He stood back a pace with a straight look on his face and spoke in a gentle manner. "Of course, Milady, I've put a lot of work into this garden and it has given me a great deal of satisfaction and pleasure over the years but I'm moving on to pastures new. I will be taking my leave at the end of this week and moving up to the Lake Side to take on the position of head gardener on a large estate."

James has never mentioned this to me; George has been here for ten years or so.

"I'm so sorry to hear that George, what has made you want to change vacation? I thought you were happy here."

"Well Milady, without seeming disrespectful I can no longer work for your husband. As much as I try nothing seems to please him and I'm not prepared to be treated with such disrespect any longer. Therefore, I gave him two weeks' notice to terminate my employment here. He firmly believes the fact that me being a tenant in his cottage gives him the right to treat and speak to me in a manner of his choosing. But being a single man with no ties he was on a wrong track and finding alternative employment was not a problem. In fact, he has done me a great favour and I'm looking forward to the new challenge ahead." It would seem James treats everyone with the same contempt.

"Well I'm truly sorry George I had no knowledge of this. It saddens me to hear you're leaving but I wish you well and good fortune on your new venture." I've always known him to be such a solid man; that James really is a bastard.

"Thank you, Milady, on the few occasions we've met you have always been so kind and polite towards me and for that I thank you." I have a lot of respect for George he's obviously a true gentleman.

"George, may I talk to you about something? Something I have never indulged to anyone else before," He looked at me with a concerned look on his face,

"Well Milady, if you wish to confide in me I'm a good listener and whatever it is you can rest assured is safe with me." Feeling a bit nervous I cleared my throat before speaking.

"Well, I'm ashamed to admit that from the very first night of being married to James he instantly changed from being the caring person who I loved and thought I knew into a controlling monster, who physically and mentally abuses me at will. As much as I try to please him it's to no avail and at times I get really frightened. I can't bring myself to mention this to my parents or even my best friend, as whenever he is in their company he comes across as the most doting, loving, and most caring husband one could ever have." The wrinkles on his brow became more intense as he frowned.

"I truly understand your concerns. I've experienced this behaviour on numerous occasions. While showing his friends around he acts the perfect gentleman, then when on his own speaks to me in a manner I don't wish to repeat." He requested for me to sit in the large arm chair in the corner of the shed as he grabbed a stool from under the bench and sat opposite me, he reached out his well weathered hand in a gesture for mine, it felt quite rough but at the same time very gentle and a sense of calm came over me as he sandwiched his other hand over mine.

"I was married for 15 years to the love of my life until she was taken from me. I have no desires to find anyone else as it wouldn't be fair to them. She was and still is my one and only true love and I can always feel her presence. That's why I never feel lonely or have the need for other company. Now listen very carefully my dear as to what I must say. Believe it or believe it not I have this gift that I never talk about. As I'm holding your hand and considering your eyes, I can see that there's someone out there with so much love to give you and who will forever protect you. No need to seek it as unbeknown to you when the time is right, this one and only true love will find you." I sat there with tears streaming down my cheeks, I so wanted to believe George but at this moment in time it would seem an impossible dream. He released my hand and smiled as he helped me out of the chair.

"So, Milady, let's go and get those flowers you came for," After picking the flowers I gave him a big thankyou hug before making my way back to the house, all the time with thoughts of his prediction.

Chapter Nine

I know I've only been with one man discounting James but what I've learnt in just that one intimate encounter has set me in good stead for the future and gave me the confidence I was sadly lacking. It helped me reach maturity as a woman and in hindsight, I now firmly believe that keeping one's virginity until married as in my case may not always be the right decision. I'm not yet clear as to what the future holds but experiencing the qualities of other men has made me realise that no man was ever going to own and control me in the way that James was trying to do, as I now believed his goal was to break menthe scary reality being, he was on the road to succeed. I would end up being a prisoner and shy recluse, only to answer to his every disposal, to be abused at will. *Well I'm sorry James, wrong answer.*

After a nice bath and change of clothes I went downstairs and into the kitchen where Edna was cleaning the stove.

"Hello Edna, I thought I'd make a pot of tea."

She stood up to fetch the kettle. "Leave it to me Milady. Where would you like me to bring it to?"

"Well how about I stay in here and we both

have a cup of tea and just enjoy a girly chat?" She went over to the cupboard and placed two cups and saucers on the kitchen table.

"Yes, that would be nice as I have to admit I'm ready for a small break." We both sat at the table and she poured the tea.

"Would you like a slice of cake as I always think tea can be a bit wet on its own."

"Oh, go on then let's indulge." We both had a giggle.

"It came as a shock to learn that George is leaving us this Friday; I had no idea until he mentioned it today."

Her face turned from a smile to sadness. "Yes Milady, I've known for some time. It's none of my business you understand but it would appear from what he said that Master James was giving him a tough time. I'm not prone to gossip but George is a very good person and nothing is ever too much trouble for him. Every day he would come to the house to see if I needed any fresh vegetables or flowers and ask if everything was all right. I for one will surely miss him."

"I have only spoken to him on a few occasions but he came across as being very obliging."

Tell me Edna, just between the two of us does

James treat you in a proper manner?"

"Well as I have mentioned before, if I do what is asked of me and without question he doesn't bother me unless it's to do with preparing food for invited guests. Plus, I do my best to stay as invisible as possible as he is not one to displease." I know exactly where she's coming from.

"Have you not married Edna? If it's not too personal."

"No Milady. I was courting a man for 3 years or so and was engaged to be married but sadly he passed away due to a serious illness. I have never bothered with any other men as he was my dearest true love and no one else could ever match up to him. But I still carry all the beautiful memories we shared together. One day I know when my time is up I will meet him on the other side where I know he will be waiting for me."

Her story was so emotional I felt a tear roll down my cheek. "Edna, my heart goes out to you and I can only admire your outlook on life."

I felt envious of couples that have a magical bond together. I thought James and I were going to be one of those but it saddened me deeply to discover that it that it wasn't meant to be. "Well Edna, it's been nice having a proper chat with you. If there's anything on your mind that you would like to talk about in the strictest confidence I'm always here."

"Thank you, Milady, that's most kind." I left the kitchen and went into the drawing room for a relaxing read before retiring for the night. As always, my thoughts distracted me. I thought about how our marriage has become loveless and about how what little time he did spend in residence was usually on his own or with his male drinking companions in the drawing room.

It was Thursday morning, my last day of freedom but there was one last thing that needed to be addressed before James arrived back the next day. After a spray of perfume and making sure I looked presentable, I made my way over to the stables. On reaching the yard I got some carrots from the feed shed and went to see Marmaduke. As I approached his stable he gave me his usual welcome and eagerly ate his treats of carrots plus an apple from my pocket. The next thing I saw was Mark walking towards me.

"Good morning Milady, will you be riding today?"

If only he knew my thoughts. "No not today thank you Mark. But if you would follow me to the tack room there is something important I need to discuss with you." We went to the tack room and closed the door. He looked a bit worried as if he thought he might be getting dismissed or something.

"Don't look so worried Mark, everything is fine. As you know my husband returns tomorrow and the girl groom starts back on Monday so before then I have one more thing to ask of you and no it's not for sex. Well that's a little bit of a lie, but afterwards, I promise never to put you in an embarrassing situation again." Feeling so sexually naive after witnessing the stable girl performing on Mark the other day it was something I needed and wanted to experience for myself.

Having secured the door so we would not to be disturbed, I went over to Mark who was looking somewhat nervous and bemused as he leaned against the bench. I went down on my knees and unfastened and his belt. I slid both his britches and boxer shorts down releasing once again this most beautifully shaft, as I clasped my hands around it's thick girth, I gazed up into his eyes.

"When ready, I want you to ejaculate into my mouth, so please don't feel you have to pull back or stop." After a few seconds of kissing and licking around the shiny head he soon had a full erection. I gently eased it into my mouth and placed my hand under his hairy sack as this was obviously something men enjoyed. As I increased my rhythm he put his hand firmly to the back of my head and started to fuck my face in unison. I must have been doing it right as within a very short time he gave out the loudest moan as his hot cum shot from the shiny head and into my mouth. He began to pull away but with it still throbbing I gently put it back until he was finished.

As I got back to my feet he pulled up his britches and fastened his belt.

"I really enjoyed doing that Mark. How was it for you? Did I do it properly?"

He looked at me completely bewildered. "Yes Milady, it was amazing but I'm confused as to why."

I looked at him and smiled. "Mark, don't let this be of concern to you. It was an experience that I needed to know and you certainly satisfied my curiosity. But now things are back to where they were, not a word must ever be spoken about our recent encounters, especially to the girl when she returns to work on Monday. Do you understand?"

He stood back speaking in a quiet tone, "If I may Milady, I would just like to say one final word. You are a very beautiful feminine lady and for whatever reasons you may have had for what has just taken place the whole experience was truly wonderful and fulfilling. You can rest assured it will remain a closely guarded secret only known to us."

I thanked him for his compliments and integrity then made my way back to the house. To my horror, I saw that James had arrived back early. Bloody hell that was a narrow escape, I had to pull myself together and act all casual. I went inside and into the drawing room.

"Hello, I wasn't expecting you until tomorrow but it's so nice to see you back as I've missed you so." I went over to him and kissed him on the cheek.

"Yes, one of the scheduled meetings had to be postponed, but where have you been for the last hour? I was looking all over the house." He looked a bit annoyed.

"I was over at the stables checking that everything was in perfect order as I do every morning." *If only he really knew how perfect it really was.*

"Good, at least it would seem you are keeping the staff in some sort of order. To change the subject, Gordon rang to say he left some papers for me to sign and during our conversation mentioned having dinner sometime soon, so I've invited him and his wife over for dinner tomorrow evening. Therefore, will you inform the house keeper and oversee the necessary arrangements." *Nice to be asked for a change,*

"I'll make sure everything is prepared and ready." He stood up from his chair behaving very master like. "Now if you'll excuse me, I have to go through to the office to catch up on some paperwork and don't wish to be disturbed. I'm sure you also have things to attend to."

With that he left the room with not so much as a 'nice to see you' or 'I missed you' Instead he just talked to me as if I was one of his staff. I went through to the kitchen where Edna was preparing lunch.

"Good morning Edna. I've just been informed by my husband that we're entertaining tomorrow evening. There will be four of us in total so would you place the settings in the dining room and have the meals ready for serving at 7.30? Also, ensure the appropriate wines are available." Wiping her hands, she stopped what she was doing and came over to me.

"Well if it's only to serve four that is no problem and I'll make sure everything is as it should be so you've no need to worry Milady. While you're here would you like to join me for a nice cup of tea? I've just made a fresh pot."

"Thank you, Edna, not while James is here but some other time I would love to."

"I understand. But you can rest assured everything tomorrow evening will be just fine."

I picked up the newspaper from the hall and went to retire to the lounge for a relaxing read all the time thinking what a lucky escape I had earlier with Mark and what an amazing experience it was. Just as I sat down that I got a phone call from my mother.

"IIi Janc, it's been a few days since we last spoke. How are things with you and James? Is he back from his business trip?"

"Yes, he came back unannounced this morning. I was expecting him back tomorrow but on my return from the stables he was already back. After only a brief encounter he went to his office asking not to be disturbed. I've just sat in the lounge reading the papers then you rang. Tomorrow evening James' accountant and his wife are coming over for dinner so I've got all the arrangements to take care of to ensure everything goes smoothly."

"Well, another reason I rang was that your father and I have been invited to attend the ball a week from Friday celebrating the engagement of Sarah Deaton's daughter to the Earl of Longford. You and James are also on the invitation list."

"Yes, I remember Sarah, she was at the same university as me studying law but finished a year before me then we lost touch. It would be lovely to see her again. I'll tell James when he's free as it would be nice to have an evening out." *Well even if he doesn't want to I will.*

"That's settled then, I'm sure there will be many other people attending that you may know. I'm quite looking forward to it as it's been a while since your father and I have had an evening out together. So, if you have a minute early next week pop over for a chat and I'll show you the invitations." *That's great news it will give me an excuse to get out.*

"I also want to have a chat with you about some other things as well so I'll give you a call Monday to arrange a time. Ok darling speak soon, Bye." I was so looking forward to the invitation but the only damper was James intense jealousy. I had to be so careful and constantly on my guard, even down to silly details like how I choose to put my makeup on.

After a couple of hours reading James returned. "I have just spoken to the house keeper and lunch will be ready in 5 minutes. I have requested it to be served in the drawing room so I suggest we make our way over now." I put down my book and followed him through. Within a few minutes, Edna brought in our lunch.

"This looks nice darling; I'm ready for a bite to eat. I thought perhaps after lunch we could go for a walk as we've not seen much of each other this week."

"I've got too much work to do and you should find something more useful to allocate your time, rather than sitting about reading. Week days are for working, weekends and evenings are for relaxing." I felt sorry for asking. I dusted myself off and then continued.

"I've spoken to the house keeper regarding the evening meal and have requested the table be laid and ready for serving at 7.30 unless she is told otherwise. By the way, speaking of entertaining, my mother rang today. We have been informally invited to attend an evening at the residence of the Earl of Longford a week from tomorrow. He is to announce the engagement of his daughter Sarah who was at the same university as me. I've not seen her since she left about 3 years ago, so it will be nice to meet up and see how she is."

He looked up at me with total disinterest. "Unfortunately, we can't attend as I will be away on business from Thursday until Saturday and the dates cannot be rearranged. And what's more I can't trust you, so you can put that idea right out of that thick skull of yours." *I've got to think of a way out of this quickly, so here goes.* "Well, the invitations came directly to my mother and father who are personal friends of the Earl and should I attend in your absence I would journey with and be chaperoned by them and seated throughout the evening at their table."

"Well in that case reluctantly you have my permission. But only on the understanding that if it became known you had conducted yourself in an improper manner there would be grave consequences. With that said I don't want it mentioned again." I couldn't believe how much he was now controlling my life, to the point that I needed permission to go out even with my own parents, but I knew he would use violence if I were to disobey him. On the other hand, I'm equally excited to be going out on my own—it feels like I'm a free liberated woman. I can dress as I please and wear what makeup I want, I can't wait for next Friday to come around.

It's been a long day, I've decide to go to my room and have a shower before going to bed. When I came out of the bath room James was sitting on the edge of the bed in his dressing gown. He must have gotten undressed rather quickly as he wasn't even in the room when I came up.

"Are you having a shower darling?" I said trying my hardest to be nice.

"No I had one earlier not as though it's any concern of yours. Now come over here I've got something for you." I went over to him and for one stupid moment I thought he had brought me something back from his business trip. How wrong I was. He grabbed hold of me and forced me face down over the side of the bed then yanked down my pyjama bottoms.

"Now as I said I've got something just for you." He leaned over spreading my legs then without any care forced himself in me. Once inside he got hold of my wrists and pulled back my arms as he started to violently fuck me, all the time talking in a degrading and aggressive manner.

"So how do you like your present bitch? Is it good? Well answer me then you fucking whore."

Although my head was still forced down on the bed I managed to mumble back,

"Yes."

As he pulled my arms back tighter, nearly pulling them out of their sockets, he shouted even louder, "Speak up bitch, I can't hear you."

I managed to turn my head slightly to one side. "Yes, yes, yes, it's really good."

He started laughing as he continued to pound me until releasing himself. After pulling out, he stepped back and spoke in a quiet tone, "There, I told you that after a while you would start to enjoy sex. It was just a matter of time, isn't that right my darling?"

Hardly able to move my arms, I got up from the bed. "Yes James, thank you. Now if you'll excuse me I have to go to the bathroom." That was so bloody painful. Fighting back the tears I went to the bathroom to get cleaned up and have another shower.

After a restless sleep, it was now 7.00am and James was already up and dressed in his suit.

"I'm off to the factory to oversee the installation of a new machine and will be back late this afternoon. All I want you to do is to make sure the house is in order and the housekeeper has everything she requires for the evening meal. Gordon and his wife will be arriving at 7.00 giving you have ample time to prepare yourself." Then without so much as a goodbye he left. Once up and dressed I made my way downstairs where Edna was in the hall putting the newspapers in the rack.

"Good morning Milady would you like me to prepare breakfast?"

"Yes, please Edna but only for one as James is out on business. Would you bring it through to the drawing room please?"

"Thank you, Milady, it will be ready in 15 minutes."

After breakfast, I walked across to the stables. As I approached Mark was grooming one of the horses on the yard, I don't know why but I was feeling a bit nervous,

"Good morning Mark, is everything ok?"

He turned towards me and smiled. "Yes, Milady everything is just fine. Will you be riding today?" I knew it was wrong but I was still having naughty thoughts about him.

"No not today, I just thought I'd give Marmaduke a bit of time and treat him to some carrots."

He put down his brushes and turned towards me. "There's a fresh sack of carrots that was delivered only yesterday. If you'll excuse me for a minute, I'll bring some over." Before I could say anything, he was gone.

"Here we are Milady, they're nice and crisp." He picked out half a dozen and placed them in a small container. He is such a caring person. As we walked over to the stable Marmaduke greeted me in his usual way.

"I've only just finished grooming him and he's now waiting to be turned out." Mark handed me some carrots and in doing so I just wanted to hold his hand. It was just so nice to have someone give me some attention in a kind and caring way.

After spending some time with my favourite horse, it was time to get back to the house but before leaving I turned towards Mark and spoke in a soft tone, "Thank you Mark."

He looked at me in a confused way. "Thank you for what Milady?" I placed my hand on his shoulder.

"Just thank you, that's all." With Mark still looking confused I made my way back over to the house.

I wasn't really looking forward to an evening with Gordon and his wife but I supposed it was a better alternative than spending a night alone with James.

It was now 5 o'clock and with no sign of James I decided to go to my room and start to get ready as I needed to wash my hair and decide what I was going to wear.

After a shower, I put on my dressing gown, went over to the dressing table, and began to dry my hair. A few moments later James entered the room and came over towards me.

"Hello darling. Has everything gone to plan at

the factory?"

"Yes, in fact it has, but more to the point, have you made all the necessary arrangements for tonight with the house keeper?"

Just like him, always looking for something to complain about. "Everything is taken care of, the dining room is set out perfectly and dinner will be served at 7.30 with wine to compliment it." He mumbled about something as he went for a shower. *It will be interesting to see how much make up Gordons wife will be wearing.* After putting on the bare basics and a very pale lipstick, it was time to get dressed. I put on a long-sleeved blouse with just the top button left undone and then a smart black knee length skirt with black shoes to match. The only jewellery I put on was a plain necklace that he had given me two years ago, so hopefully there's no reason to complain about how I look or what I'm wearing.

James came into the bedroom and made his way over to where I was sitting and all the time his eyes were fixed on my appearance. I began to speak in a positive tone.

"I'm looking forward to meeting Gordon and his wife. I've only spoken to her a few times and it would be nice to know her better."

He looked at me with contempt. "She is a

highly intelligent woman and you would do well to take note of what she has to say. You might even learn something but I very much doubt it. Now if you're done up here I suggest you go down and have a final check with the housekeeper to ensure we are ready to welcome our guests. If there are any mishaps, I'll personally hold you to account."

What a bastard. But I thought myself fortunate that he didn't disapprove on how I looked again.

Just to be on the safe side I had a final check in the dining room then onto the kitchen where I was reassuring by Edna that all was well and on track, I really don't know how she runs this house, she's worth her weight in gold. The doorbell rang. *Surely it can't be them this early at 6 o'clock.* I opened the door, it was George the gardener.

I smiled at him and spoke in a quiet tone, "Hello George, what can I do for you?"

"Well Milady, I've come to collect my P45 together with two weeks owed pay and then I will take my leave."

"If you'll excuse me for a moment I'll get my husband, he attends to all these matters." I went upstairs and informed James that the gardener wished to see him.

"I have no need or desire to speak with him

he's been dismissed from his duties and is vacating the cottage. Go down to my office where you will find a large brown envelope on my desk with a Mr. G Reynolds written on it. Inside is all the necessary paperwork including his final earning but before you hand him the envelope ensure he gives you the keys to the cottage." I went down to his office, picked up the envelope and took it out to George.

"Here you are, but before I hand it over I've been instructed that you must hand over the keys to the cottage." He did as I requested and I handed him the envelope.

Before he was about to leave I leaned forward and whispered to him, "I wish you good George in all you do."

A huge smile beamed across his rugged face as he leaned forward and whispered, "Now remember what I said the other day" He then raised his hand to bid farewell. As I went back into the house James was nearing the bottom of the hall stairs and had an annoyed look on his face.

"That took some time; what was all that about?"

Closing the door, I turned towards him and spoke back in a stern manner, "Well would you believe he had the audacity to say he would forward the keys after he had checked the contents of the envelope. I immediately informed him that my husband does not make errors and assured him everything would be present and correct. With that said he handed the keys over; what an insolent man."

James looked at me a bit bemused, "The darn cheek of the man. As you quite rightly said I do not make errors and you acted accordingly. Perhaps now at last you're learning how to treat employees." That's a one up for me. With him now believing I have total disregard for the staff he has little or no reason ever to suspect otherwise.

A short time later Gordon and his wife arrived. After greeting them and taking their coats we went through to the lounge and poured some drinks. Before sitting down, I went to the kitchen and informed Edna that the guests had arrived and to confirm that dinner would be served at 7.30. With everything going as planned I returned to the lounge.

Chapter Ten

Once back in the lounge I picked up my glass of wine and spoke to Caroline. "This is only the third time we have met, are you involved in Gordon's business?"

She looked at me with a frown on her face. "My dear girl, one can't imagine anything more vulgar than sifting through piles of paperwork. I make better use of my time organising activities for the local church and the round table."

I thought pardon one for asking. "If you don't mind me asking how do you utilise your time?" I wanted to say *"I fuck the groom!"* but somehow, I don't think that would go down too well.

"A lot of my time is taken up ensuring the house and estate is functioning properly and if I get some spare time I go riding on my favourite horse or I may even go into town and meet up with my friend for a coffee and a bit of shopping." *I don't think judging by the look on her face that she was very impressed.*

After a few drinks, we went to the dining room for dinner. Edna had really done us proud. During the meal, it wasn't long before Caroline piped up again, "Do you accompany James when on his business trips? I frequently do with Gordon, don't I dear?" Gordon just looked over and nodded in acknowledgement.

"No not yet," *And I don't suppose I ever will, as that would spoil his shagging habits.*

"Well perhaps when you're more mature in the business world and know how to conduct yourself I'm sure James would give it some consideration. What say you James?"

He began to chuckle as he turned towards us. "Of course, I would, I was only thinking this very day that it would be nice to have my precious wife travel alongside me as I do miss her so when I'm away. Isn't that right darling?" He looked directly in my eye as if to say *don't you dare contradict me.*

"Yes, I do miss him and at times it can get a bit lonely as I'm sure it does for James but I understand his work is very important and I wouldn't want to be in the way." Gordon spoke out as he clapped his hands.

"Well said that woman. James, you are indeed a lucky man to have such an understanding wife." "Indeed, I am, she is very precious and I'm so proud to have her as my wife and look forward too many happy years together." *You lying bastard.* Gordon rose his glass and said,

"Well Jane and James, first I would like to

thank you for inviting us over for a splendid meal. And secondly, I would like us to raise our glasses in a toast to a wonderful couple. May you have many happy and fruitful years together. Cheers."

Although this sham toast was a load of bullshit, Caroline had to use all of her will power to raise her glass as she was clearly miffed at not being the centre of attention.

After dinner and a few more drinks the evening ended and we bid farewell to Gordon and his wife as they set off for home. Leaving James to lock up I made my way up to bed. After changing into my bed clothes, I sat at the dressing table to brush my hair and remove what little make up I had on.

Moments later James entered the room.

"I think the evening went very well. I really enjoyed their company. It was nice to have a chat with Caroline and get to know her better,"

He got up from the bed and came over to the dressing table. For a few seconds, he just stood there in silence then grabbed hold of my hair and yanked my head back.

"Don't ever try to upstage me in front of my friends again bitch with your fucking smart talk about being lonely trying to make me feel guilty."

I tried to hold back my tears. "I was only trying

to portray my affection for you and would never want to do you wrong." He threw my head forward with such force it hit the mirror at the rear of the dressing table.

"Please James, why do you treat me this way when I do my utmost to please you?" He grabbed hold of me again, pulling me off the stool.

"So, you're really doing your utmost to please me, are you?"

He pulled me up and stood in front of me. "Well let's put this fucking theory of yours to the test, now take of those pyjamas." I did as he asked standing naked dreading what might be coming next. He then scattered everything that was on the dressing table on to the floor. "Right, now sit on the table with your legs spread and don't say a word." As I sat on the table he removed his clothes and then stood between my thighs, placing my hand on his semi hard penis.

"Now rub this." Within a few seconds of me touching him he had an instant erection then moved in closer.

"So, do you think you're pleasing me bitch? Well I've got something to please you." With both hands tightly gripping my legs he pulled me down onto him. I cried aloud as he rammed it in me but that only spurned him on as he began to fuck me so hard that the dressing table began to bang loudly against the wall. Thankfully again it was short lived. He released himself then pulled back in the belief that he was the world's greatest lover and spoke as if he had just done me a great favour, "Tell me darling, did that please and satisfy you? Only I thought you would like to try something different." I eased myself off the table and put back on my pyjamas.

"Yes, darling very much so. I believe the man should be the dominant force and you're such a strong experienced lover. You know just how to please a woman." It wasn't the answer I had in mind but it was the right one to satisfy this egotistical bastard and save me from a serious beating.

"Thank you my precious, I always aim to please. Now off you go to the bathroom to make yourself presentable."

I was feeling concerned and very frightened. In the past few weeks the physical side of his abuse had become more intense. I fear that one day soon he may beat me again. I am not sure yet what my options are for escaping.

No matter what I may say to the contrary it's impossible for me to prove otherwise as all the abuse takes place in the house and mainly in the bedroom. It is something he would most strenuously deny, making me out to be the evil one. It's almost certain people from the outside including my parents would take his side.

After a long and tedious week, I was feeling happy as it was now Thursday and James was about to leave on his business trip, leaving me free for the rest of the day. Plus, I have the excitement of going to the dance tomorrow without him spying on me and the usual confrontation when we get back. Before leaving he came into the lounge where I was reading the newspaper.

He put down his briefcase and then clasped my jaw firmly with his left hand while looking straight into my eyes. "Now don't forget bitch what I said regarding your little escapade tomorrow night. If I hear even the slightest mention of any inappropriate behaviour you will stay confined to your room always unless I say otherwise, do you understand?" Increasing his vice-like grip he pushed my head right back, "I'll ask you one more fucking time: do you understand?"

"Yes of course James, I promise."

He released his grip and stepped back. "I know you will darling, just needed to clarify the situation, that's all." He picked up his briefcase, bent over and kissed me on the forehead and then left. On hearing his car head off down the drive I sat back in the chair and gave a huge sigh of relief.

I went to the kitchen to make myself a nice strong coffee. It was nice just to have the kitchen to myself. I spoke too soon though because as I was about to leave Edna entered.

"You should have let me do that for you Milady, that's what I'm here for and less I forget have you a spare key to the office? Only the door was left open, Master James must have been in a hurry as he always makes sure it's securely locked."

"No I haven't but thank you for bringing it to my attention. I'm sure there's no need for concern as he always leaves everything secure and anything of value will be in the safe." I continued through to the lounge to enjoy my coffee and finish reading the newspapers.

Curiosity was getting the better of me so on the pretence of checking that nothing of value was in view I gingerly crept into his office and very quietly closed the door behind me. Even though he was away I still felt extremely nervous. Tip toeing over to his huge highly polished oak desk, I carefully and slowly opened some of the drawers only to find lots of paper related to his work. On the left-hand side of the desk was a small narrow drawer with the key still in the lock. As I opened it I saw that there were many partitions containing pens and other related writing items but just as I was about to close it I noticed a small thin silver box, I couldn't resist but when removing the lid, I gasped in horror and nearly dropped it, for the cards inside were all from female escorts. Two of them had an additional personal number written on them by hand. Shaking like a leaf, I closed the lid and put the box back in the exact place I found it then made a swift exit. It was now clear that even whilst courting and long before we got married he was shagging around. Unfortunately, I daren't confront him as he would know I've been nosing around in his desk and that would most certainly end up with extreme consequences.

On a happier note, I went up to my room to go through my clothes and find something nice and feminine to wear for tomorrow night. After deciding, I checked through my make up only to discover my favourite red lipstick was badly damaged when that bastard rubbed it all over my face in a fit of anger. As it's only mid-day I decided to nip into town and buy another one but this time I will hide it so he's none the wiser. Tomorrow night I want to feel and look extra special and not the dowdy dull woman he portrays me to be.

It was finally Friday and I was so excited, the same feeling as when I was a teenager going out to my first dance. I couldn't believe I was going out on my own. Before I do anything else it's time for a bit of breakfast and a nice cup of tea. As usual Edna was in the kitchen pottering about.

"Good morning Edna. I would just fancy some breakfast and a pot of tea."

"Well Milady you just leave it to me. There's nothing better than a full hearty breakfast to see you through the day and may I say you're looking very happy."

"Yes, I'm attending an engagement party this evening for one of my close college friends but unfortunately I will be going on my own as James is away on business."

She looked at me and smiled as if she knew things weren't right between us. "Never mind, I'm sure you will have a great time being amongst your friends."

"Yes, it will be like a reunion. When ready I'll take breakfast in the drawing room."

"Very well Milady." On my way to the dining room I picked up the morning papers to catch up on the latest news.

After breakfast, I got changed and went to the stables to take Marmaduke out for a ride. Mark wasn't around so I tacked him myself and went for a nice hack. It was great spending some quality time together.

When we got back Mark was in the yard and came over to greet us.

"Morning Malady, if I knew you were going out I would have tackled him up ready."

"Thank you, it was a last-minute decision but you can help me with his saddle and finish things off if you would, as I'm a bit pushed for time."

"Leave it with me Milady, I'll make sure he's cleaned and groomed before going to his stable." It's still hard to stop my eyes from glancing down to his tight britches.

"Thank you, Mark, will talk later." I left him to it. Now back to the house to start to getting ready for tonight. Having had a full breakfast, I decided to skip lunch and go to my room as I had to shower, wash my hair, and take my time to prepare myself ready for tonight.

It was near time to leave, but as I was putting on my favourite red lipstick I still felt nervous thinking James would walk in at any minute even though he was away. I picked up my bag and took one last look in the mirror. Pleased with how I looked then I hastily made my exit from the house.

On arrival at my parents' my mother came over

to greet me. "Hello darling, you look absolutely gorgeous. That was great timing as your father is about to bring the car around." A few moments later as the car pulled up and I requested my mother to sit in the front. As I sat the rear my father turned around towards me.

"Hello my dearest, you're looking very smart. It's a shame that James couldn't make it tonight but I'm sure there will be many people you know to mingle with. So, let's go and have an enjoyable evening." *Yes, what a shame that James isn't here.*

Chapter Eleven

On arriving we were greeted by a very smart footman who then asked for our invitation card. Once confirmed he called out our names and politely welcomed us in. The huge hall was full of guests and a waiter approached us with a tray of drinks.

My father put up his hand to acknowledge someone he had seen across the room. "If you'll just excuse us for a moment there are two friends of ours over there that we haven't seen for quite some time. In the meantime, you can meet up with Sarah and reminisce with your other friends. We'll catch up with you later."

So here I am, standing in this vast hall full of people and feeling a little intimidated as it would appear that most are with partners. While pretending to mingle in the crowd I noticed Sarah who was no more than ten feet away.

As I made my way over she in turn saw me and came over to greet me with a big hug. "Hello Jane, it's so lovely to see you and many thanks for coming tonight. I can't believe so many people are here."

"Well Sarah, you look amazing and congratulations on your engagement. When you left university, somehow we lost contact but it's lovely to see you again." *I just hope her marriage turns out to be a lot better than mine is.*

"I've got a lot of people to see tonight but before the evening ends lets swap phone numbers so we can meet up one morning for a coffee and chat as I'm sure we have a lot of catching up to do."

"Yes, that would be great. I'll catch up with you later. "The strange thing is I hardly recognise anyone. Feeling like a bit like a fish out of water I decided to go and powder my nose.

Just as I was about to turn around this deep velvety voice spoke from behind, "Good evening Lady Jane." I had only met him the one time but would recognise that voice anywhere. With my legs trembling I slowly turned around and there was the most beautiful man I have ever laid eyes on. There, towering over me was Captain Phillips. I took a deep breath as I tried to compose myself.

"Good evening kind sir, have we met somewhere before?" As if I didn't know, how the bloody hell could any woman forget meeting such a beautiful man?

"Well perhaps you may recall the recent dinner dance held by Lord and Lady Benson. Towards the end of the evening I had the pleasure of dancing with the most beautiful elegant lady, my main disappointment being that it was far too brief." Is he coming onto me? I'm feeling a bit nervous now as I don't really know who knows who here, or whether James sent a plant to spy on me. I certainly wouldn't put it past the devious bastard.

"Oh, yes how silly of me. It was the Excuse Me Waltz and you came in towards the end. So, what brings you here this evening? Are you friends with Sarah?"

"I only met Sarah when she started dating Richard, my long-standing friend. I couldn't wish for him to meet a nicer person. I sincerely wish them all the best. Would I be right in saying Sarah is your friend?"

"Yes, she is, we were at college together but lost touch when she left and then from unexpected I got an invite for tonight via my parents, who by the way are here somewhere talking with old friends."

"Please forgive me as I don't wish to pry, but you appeared to seem a little lost amongst these people."

"Is it that obvious? But yes, you're right I came with my parents as my husband is away on business. I've spoken to Sarah but apart from her I hardly recognise anyone."

"Well you're not exactly on your own as there

are several guests that I've never seen acquainted with. But if you'll allow me, my good friend Richard has just come into view and I would like to introduce you to him." His height allowed him to spot anyone within view. A few moments later we met up with his friend.

"Richard, I would like to introduce you to Lady Jane, who is a long-term college friend of Sarah." He smiled as we shook hands.

"Pleased to make your acquaintance, you do realise you're the envy of every woman here being at the side of the most handsome eligible bachelor on the planet."

The captain turned towards me as they chuckled together. "Now you see what a mischief he is." But I must agree with Richard. He must have many female admirers, me being one of them. We were then interrupted by the master of ceremonies over the PA system.

"My Lords, Ladies and gentlemen, please may I have your attention. The buffet is now open in the dining hall and would everyone kindly ensure their glasses are ready for the toast, soon to be announced. Thank you."

"May I escort you through to the buffet and be so bold as to sit at your table?" How could I refuse such an offer, I feel like a million dollars walking beside this man and as stupid as it may seem I feel safe and protected. What's more, even if any of this got back to James it would be worth a good hiding.

"Thank you, I would like to accept your kind offer." We made our way to the most amazing buffet you could ever imagine. After filling our plates, we managed to find a table in the corner of the room. Once sat down opposite each other he smiled towards me, showing the most perfect set of white teeth.

"Please don't think of me as being forward but I would like you to address me by my first name Andrew, as do all my friends. May I in turn be so bold as to do the same with you?"

I feel a tremble whilst trying to compose myself. "Yes, I'm comfortable with that. You may call me Jane but only within our own private company."

He leaned slightly forward and whispered, "Very well Jane, this will be just our little secret." I smiled and nodded in approval. "Per what your friend Richard implied, would I be right to assume that you're not attached to anyone." This was surprising to me, as I'm sure he could have the pick of any woman he desired.

"Well since you asked I do have lady friends but not in the romantic sense as it were. My career takes me all over the world and wouldn't deem it fair to be away for several months at a time if I were in a serious relationship."

What an honourable man, very different from my husband who enjoys spending as much time away as he can. Just as I was getting to know him a little better the emcee made an announcement.

"My Lords, Ladies and Gentlemen I give you the Earl of Longford." He came to the microphone and spoke for a few moments before announcing the engagement of his beloved daughter Sarah to his future son-in-law Richard. After raising our glasses and the applause, everyone continued what they were doing.

"Unfortunately, my husband spends a lot of time away on business, mainly abroad and at times the days can be very long." I hope I'm not giving him the wrong impression by discussing details regarding my personal life.

As he leaned slightly forward he spoke in a very soft and gentle tone, "Jane, you are a very beautiful and slightly mysterious Lady with a smile that can melt a man's heart. But by looking deep into those piercing blue eyes and please forgive me for saying, I can't help but detect a touch of sadness." I just wanted to reach out and hold his hand.

"No not at all. It's been a long and busy day; just feel a bit tired that's all." I didn't think it was that obvious but he was so right.

"I'm so sorry, I was truly out of order to have suggested such a thing."

"Not at all, I'm impressed with your powers of observation. Please don't turn around as my mother is heading over in this direction so let's discuss something more topical like Sarah and Robert's engagement.

"Hello Mother. Let me introduce you to Captain Phillips, a close friend of Robert and Sarah."

He very politely stood up to greet her. "Pleased to make your acquaintance, we were discussing the engagement and what a grand couple they make."

My mother looked up at him in awe as he was so tall. "Likewise, I'm sure; it's been a most enjoyable evening." She then turned her attention towards me. "Unfortunately, your father has no desire to stay when the dancing begins as he seems to think it's for the younger generation. So, could you make your way to the entrance in approximately 5 minutes? Once again pleased to meet you Captain," She turned away and made her way across the room.

"That is so unfortunate, I was hoping we may have had a dance together as the last one I recall ended so abruptly."

I knew how he felt as I felt the same way. "Yes, I would also like to have a dance but perhaps it wasn't meant to be, as it might look improper me being a married lady in an embrace with a single gentleman on the dance floor." Just the thought of us being together in such proximity brought me out in goose bumps.

"It was nice of you to come to my aid tonight Andrew. I've really enjoyed your company but now I have to take my leave as my parents will be waiting." We both stood up from the table and smiled at each other.

"You have made my evening Jane, perhaps our paths may cross again." *I do hope so*. "Yes, perhaps they might. Goodnight Andrew." As I walked away I couldn't resist a backward glance and he was still focused on me as we smiled and waved farewell.

Chapter Twelve

As I got in the car my father turned towards me, "Your Mother tells me you had the pleasure of meeting Captain Phillips. Pay attention he is the most honourable upstanding professional gentleman anyone could ever wish to meet and a true credit to his uniform." I felt sick to my stomach knowing that he was still back there and I was on my way back to that lonely empty house. I knew the situation was impossible and that I should now put him out of my mind but I couldn't get rid of the feeling I was left with. It had gone right down to my soul. It was one that I'd never experienced before, perhaps when I wake in the morning my head will have cleared.

I just arrived back home from my parents and went upstairs to my room. After removing my makeup and getting cleaned up I got into bed and picked up my book. Of course, Andrew was still entrenched in my mind so turned off the light and drifted off to sleep.

I must have slept well as it was 9 in the morning, time to get up. After a shower, I made my way downstairs for breakfast and asked Edna to bring it through to the drawing room. I picked up the papers on my way through for a quiet read but just as I settled a car pulled up the drive, it was

James.

I went to the front door to greet him. "Hello darling, you've timed that just right; The house keeper is preparing breakfast,"

"Not for me, I've already had mine at the hotel." *Yes, and I bet that wasn't the only thing that you had at that hotel.* That was the sum of our conversation before he disappeared upstairs.

After my breakfast, I went to get changed as I wanted to take out my horse for some exercise. When I entered my room, James was in the shower so I had a quick look at his clothes. His shirt reeked of perfume, making it obvious what he had been up to.

As I was getting changed into my jodhpurs James came into the room.

"I'm just going to take Marmaduke for a short ride, will you join me? We haven't been out for a ride together lately."

My suggestion just was ignored. "No, I've things to attend to and before I forget we have been invited over for drinks tonight with Gordon and his wife. So, have yourself ready for 6 o'clock sharp." He then disappeared back into the bathroom. As I made my way over to the stables it seemed strange that he never questioned me about last night but I feel sure he will.

I really enjoyed my time with Marmaduke but also enjoyed reminiscing about my time spent with Andrew last night. Soon it was time I made my way back to the house. The last thing on my mind was having drinks with Gordon and that stuck-up wife of his, but had no choice in the matter.

After a late lunch, I went up to my room for a shower and to sort out something suitable to wear for tonight. I began to get ready and fear gripped me as it usually does when I perform this task. About an hour later James entered the room and went to the bathroom.

I was sitting at my dressing table putting on my make up when he opened the bathroom door shouting and yelling, "Where's my bloody comb? It was on the shelf this morning what have you done with it?"

I turned around and spoke in a soft tone, "I don't know darling, I haven't seen it. Even if I had would have no reason to move it." I could see the rage building up in his eyes.

"So, you haven't seen it, then perhaps I'd better look elsewhere." He went over to the sideboard and pulled out every single drawer, tipping the contents all over onto the floor and then came over to where I was sitting and snarled at me. "Has that jogged your memory as to where you've put it?"

Feeling terrified, I didn't know what to say or do except try and stay calm. "I honestly haven't seen or touched your comb but it's no problem. Here, you can use one of mine and I'll look for yours later. It can't be far away."

"You just don't get it, do you? I don't want to use your fucking filthy comb! Get out of my way bitch." He hit me so hard across the side of my face it knocked me clean off my stool and onto the floor. Not content with that, he pulled out the two drawers of the dressing table and tipped the contents directly over me.

He bent down and grabbed me by the hair, pulling me up as I was screaming. He pinned me hard against the wall and spoke in the evillest tone, "Now then you fucking waste of space, I will be going without you tonight and will merely say your absence is due to you feeling unwell. I will send your apologies. In the meantime, you will clear up this mess that you have instigated and on my return this room will be immaculate. What's more you had better find that comb. Is that clear your useless bitch?"

It was hard to hear much of what he was saying as I had this loud ringing noise in my ear where he had struck me but I managed to mumble an answer,

"Yes I'll make sure." With that evil look in his eyes and still holding my hair, he pulled me sideways,

"Just one word of advice before I leave, if you mention or report this to anyone or have any thoughts of leaving I will track you down like a fucking dog and kill you." He then punched me so hard on the other side of my face that I crashed to the floor.

I'm not sure how long it was before I came around and managed to get on my feet, but once I was up I made my way to the bathroom. Looking in the mirror I couldn't believe what he had done to me. Both cheeks were bright red and badly swollen as was my left eye but my bottom lip was hurting the most and was still bleeding profusely from being cut on my teeth. I cleaned myself up as best I could and knew I had to get the room back in order. I felt so scared and now feared for my life. Just as I was picking up the drawers of my dressing table there was a knock at the door. I gingerly made my way over expecting the worst and slowly opened it only to see Edna standing there. I went down on my knees and burst into tears, Edna knelt to embrace me.

"What on earth has as he done to you Milady? Just look at you and the state of this room! I was just about to finish my shift and retire to my quarters when I heard someone scream out. As no one else was in the house I knew it could only be you. I heard your husband shouting and then a few moments later I saw him storm off alone in his car. I know it isn't my business to interfere but as everything went so quiet I was concerned for your wellbeing. I'm so glad I came up! You must see a doctor at once and seriously consider calling the police." *I daren't do that. It would only make things worse.*

"No Edna it's all right. I will be just fine. You get off; you've already done your days' work."

She closed the door and helped me over to the large chair in the corner of the room and sat me down. "Now then Milady, this is woman to woman and has nothing to do with work. I'm not leaving you here in this condition to clean up this mess. We will do it together. All you have to do is instruct me in what order and where things go and we'll have it back exactly as it was in no time at all."

I don't think I could have done this without Edna. Within an hour, she had everything back in place and had even cleaned the bathroom where I had been bleeding.

"Edna, I can't even begin to thank you for your help and kindness."

She came over and sat beside me and held my hand. "As I've said before Milady it's not my place to interfere but I know he doesn't treat you properly. What bit of advice I can offer is that you seriously consider your position here? Now before I leave I'm going to make us a nice cup of tea and I won't take no for an answer."

She let go of my hand and left the room. My face felt like it was on fire and my lip was so tender. I sat at my dressing table and tried to make myself look more presentable but there wasn't much I could do. A few moments later Edna came back with a tray. We sat talking for a while but before she left she reassured me that if I needed her to just knock on her door.

Laying on the bed still fully clothed, I must have dozed off but was woken by a loud banging on the front door. It was 1 o'clock in the morning. My body was racked with pain as I got up and made my way downstairs. My first thought was that he had forgotten his key and was locked out—I was probably in for another beating.

As I gingerly opened the door; stood in front of me were two burly police officers. I froze on the spot. *Bloody hell, Edna must have called them.*

"Yes Officers, is there something I can help you with? Only it is rather late."

"May we come inside for a moment?"

They virtually invited themselves in and closed the door and then one of them spoke in a very solemn tone. "Before I say anything else Madam, is there anything you wish to tell me regarding the bruising around your face and blood splattered clothes?" I must have looked like something from a horror movie

"No officer, everything is fine, I've just had a bit of an accident. So please tell me the purpose of your visit"

"Well I'm sorry to have to ask you this but for identification purposes would your name be Lady Jane, wife of James Handley?"

"Yes, that is correct. Now would you mind explaining what's this all about?"

"I am sorry to inform you that your husband has been in an accident and is in a life-threatening condition. It is also my duty to inform you that the unidentified female passenger that was also in the front of the vehicle was pronounced dead on arrival at the scene. The vehicle skidded of the road and hit a tree, at this stage of the investigation we believe no other parties were involved."

"Oh, my god, where is he now?"

"At the Royal Infirmary Canterbury, we can take you if wish."

"No thank you, I will take myself there and will leave in a few moments." Once more they gave their apologies and left.

As I turned around Edna came into the hall. "What is it Milady? I haven't reported him to the Police for his wrong doing."

"I know Edna. James has had an accident and apparently is in a critical condition but the woman who was with him is dead. So, I'm just on my way to the hospital to find out exactly what has taken place." I'm intrigued to know who the mystery woman is.

"You're in no fit state to be out on your own at this late hour, please let me accompany you to the hospital as I can wait in reception." I was so grateful for her kindness and help tonight.

"Thank you, Edna. I would very much appreciate that. I'll bring the car around but please hurry as we must leave at once."

When we arrived at the hospital Edna made her way to the waiting room while I headed off to reception. Having explained who, I was, the receptionist escorted me down a long corridor and into a room where the same two policemen were together with a doctor and nurse.

The doctor came over and spoke, "The

condition of your husband is grave. He is unlikely to survive the night and at best if he does he will be paralysed from the neck down and will need 24-7 around the clock care."

"This is such a shock but I'm somewhat bewildered about the woman who was with him because I was under the impression he was at his friend's house. Could someone please enlighten me?"

One of the officers got to his feet. "Well I'm unable to give you her personal details at this stage of our investigation but I can inform you that when we attended the scene your husband was found to be unconscious still in the driver's seat with some of his clothing partly removed and the lady in question was found in the foot well by his feet. It would appear she was performing some form of sexual activity and while possibly being distracted he lost control and swerved into a tree. Sorry for being so blunt but as unpleasant as it may be, I must declare and state the facts exactly as we found them. The coroner will have the full report relating to the cause of death of the said woman and the police report as to the cause of the accident within the next seven days."

This is just too much to take in. The police officers and the doctor left leaving me with the nurse. After hearing, what had just been said I was left with a feeling of shame and humiliation but she was genuinely sympathetic towards me.

"I don't wish to intrude but it looks as though you've been in some type of accident as your face is very bruised and swollen and there's a nasty gash on your lip." *Fuck it, why should I cover up for that bastard after how he has just humiliated me?*

"Well I am now going to confess it was my husband that inflicted these injuries before he left to go out this evening. I now wish to press charges against him." The nurse stood straight as she adjusted her uniform.

"I'm sure you have made the right decision but before you leave please come and see me and I will give you something to reduce the swelling and relieve the pain. Your husband is drifting in and out of consciousness but if you wish I can take you to see him. He's in the intensive care room at the end of the corridor, being the last door on your right. If you would follow me I can take you down."

"I'm not sure I want to see him right now as I would like to go for a coffee first and see my friend who is waiting in reception", I thanked her and made my way to find Edna. She was sitting quietly reading a magazine. "Hi Edna I'm afraid the situation is very serious. He is paralysed for the rest of his life from the neck down." She held my hand as I sat beside her and while explaining what had happened in the car per the police findings I burst into tears.

"Well Milady, as bad as it appears there's nothing you can do to change the situation and you have nothing to be ashamed of, nothing at all, do you hear? He is the guilty one, not you."

"Yes, I know Edna. I don't ever want to see him again but I've got to, as I would never forgive myself if he passed away before hearing my final words." I made my way down the corridor and gingerly entered his room. He looked unconscious and was heavily bandaged with tubes down both nostrils to help with his breathing. I nervously pulled up a chair and sat beside him. Even though he was bed-ridden I was still frightened of him.

Chapter Thirteen

After about twenty minutes he started to come around. Still with that contemptuous look in his eye he turned towards me and whispered in a breathy voice, "I knew you would be here my darling, my body feels like a lead weight and I can only move my head so you're going to have to take care for me until I recover."

After what he's just put me through, talk about bloody arrogant. "Well James my darling, listen carefully as to what I'm going to say. The police have informed me that the woman who was in the front of the car with you was probably in the act of sucking your cock, and that's why you lost control and crashed into a tree. Unfortunately, she died of her injuries. Also, the surgeon who is attending you has informed me that if you do survive the next 24 hours you will remain paralysed for the rest of your life from the neck down. You may also be surprised that I have been in your desk that you carelessly left unlocked only to find all the escort girlfriends that entertain you on your many so called business trips. So, overall at this very moment in time you don't have a lot going for you." Even though he was paralysed his eyes were that of a raging bull. He started spluttering while violently moving his head from side to side as if he wanted to lash out and strike me.

I leaned over, stared into his raging eyes and whispered in his ear, "You can't hurt me anymore you fucking bastard. So, listen very carefully, just three more things I'm going to say before you will never see or hear from me again. One; if you do survive you can rant and rave till you're blue in the face but there's no way on God's earth I will forfeit my life to care for a rotten to the core bastard like you. Two; you thought you were a stud in the bedroom but in truth, you're the most pathetic lover on this planet. Three; being the most important, whatever you're going through right now could never ever compensate for the physical and mental torture that you have inflicted on me from the very first day we were married and sincerely I hope you die and rot in hell. Goodbye James." I got up from my chair and without even a glance back left the room and him forever.

Back in reception I went over to Edna. "I've seen and spoken to him. Tomorrow I will be moving out of the house and his life, never wanting to see or hear from ever him again. I will be looking for alternative accommodation and moving out as soon as possible."

"I'm so pleased that you have had the courage Milady. This is now the time to move on and seek a better life. I also will be leaving this household and will stay with my sister until I find another post."

When we arrived back at the house Edna went to her quarters. For me it wasn't worth going to bed. As it would be daylight in an hour so I made a drink and sat in the lounge with a thousand and one thoughts going through my head. I knew it was still quite early but I decided to ring my mother. I hardly had a chance to say much as all she said was "I'm on my way over," and put the phone down. It wasn't long before both my parents were at the front door.

As I opened it my mother gasped in horror. "What has happened to my baby, just look at your face?" Tears were rolling down my cheeks as she hugged me, never was I so glad to see my mum.

"Come in and I will try and explain what had happened." We went into the lounge and I told them the reason he got angry and then hit me and that it was just one of many times he had assaulted me since we were married.

After telling them about the accident and the detailed police account as to what caused it, my father just about blew a fuse.

"Now listen to me young lady, I will not tolerate such behaviour towards my daughter and you must leave this house immediately. Now pack what is rightfully yours and I will arrange the appropriate transport to bring your belongings back to our house where you will stay for if you deem fit." He came over to me and for the first time in years embraced me and spoke in a gentle tone, "You're safe now my child; your mother and I will never let any harm come to you again."

Just as they were about to leave the phone rang, it was the hospital. I looked over towards my parents. "He has just passed away."

I started to cry but not for him. Finally, the shackles had been removed and I was a free woman. The one comforting moment for me was that I had the courage to tell him my true feelings before he met his maker.

My father came back over to me. "I have never wished evil on any man but this was entirely of his doing and he has now paid the ultimate price. Now let's put this behind us and move on to the future." I got a few things together and went back to my parents as I could never stay in that house ever again.

The next day I went back over to start packing my things. On arriving Edna came over to greet me, "Good morning Milady, have there been any further updates from the hospital?"

"Yes, Edna I'm afraid there has. He passed away in the early hours I'm here to get all my belongings together and sent over to my parents where I will be staying until I make alternative arrangements. But please don't worry, you can stay if you wish and I will make sure you are paid in full as with all the other staff."

"Thank you, Milady. Just to keep things in order I will work a week's notice and then will be moving in with my sister. But I will leave a forwarding address and phone number should you wish to contact me." I went over and gave her a hug.

"Thank you, Edna, but please come and see me before you leave." I made my way upstairs and into the bedroom. It felt weird and the room was deadly silent. It's hard to imagine that within such a short period I went from being a happy single woman to an abused married woman and now a widow. I wasn't quite sure where to go from there but I needed a few weeks to clear my head before making any decisions. I sat down at my dressing table and looked in the mirror. I was going to be house bound for at least another two days. My left eye was still bruised and swollen as was my bottom lip, a chilling reminder me of that bastard. In a fit of anger, I pulled the mirror bizarre and smashed it to a thousand pieces on the floor. I knew it didn't change anything but it made me feel better.

After packing, a few clothes, and personal

affects I set off to my parent's house. On announcing my arrival, I took my things up to my room. As I was sorting my clothes out my father came in and put his arm around my shoulder.

"I know it might be a silly question but how are you feeling?"

"I'm ok father, just a bit weary and messed up not knowing what to do next."

"Well Jane my precious, there's no need to worry about a thing I will help you with all the unpleasant arrangements regarding the estate and financial matters and be with you all the way."

I gave him a great big hug and thanked him and after he left I sat down and gave a huge sigh of relief. That lifted such a weight off my mind and I no longer felt that I was on my own.

True to his word my father helped me with all the arrangements and appointments regarding the estate such as visiting the bank and solicitors. In his will, it turned out that his one and only brother who unbeknown to me was also his business partner was to inherit the mansion and his personal wealth. A few months later his brother moved into the manor and took over the estate. I had never met him before but he seemed a nice gentleman. But then again so did his brother. Perhaps it's not fair to judge someone based on that assumption.

My father was furious and wanted me to act and contest the will but I didn't want anything from his estate as it would just be a reminder of the past. I just wanted to put it all behind me and lay it to rest.

Chapter Fourteen

Six months had passed since that dreadful night and I now felt confident enough to get my life back on track. I had just bought a nice apartment in Canterbury overlooking the park and my beloved horse is in a livery yard just two miles away.

Being a qualified lawyer I have restarted my career and joined a team of local solicitors. I regularly meet up with my best friend Samantha as she also works in Canterbury. One Saturday morning about 9 pm the phone rang and I got the shock of my life. I trembled as I instantly recognised the voice on the other end, it was Captain Andrew.

"Hello Jane, how are you?"

Trying to compose myself I took a deep breath. "Hi Andrew, this is a pleasant surprise, I'm very well thank you, I was just about to do a bit off shopping." I wanted to sound as if everything was normal.

"Sorry to ring you at an inappropriate moment, perhaps I may call you later?" *Why did I have to open my big mouth?* "No, it's nothing important, nice to hear from you. Is everything good with you?"

"Yes, I'm fine thank you, Jane. I don't wish to dwell on the past but I was deeply hurt and concerned when I was just recently made aware of the past events that occurred in your life. I can't imagine what hell you must have endured and I commend you on your dignity and bravery."

"Thank you, Andrew. It was pretty ghastly but I'm now keeping busy with my career and moving on with my life."

"Well done and good for you. Hopefully on a brighter note, may I be so bold as to ask if we could meet up for a coffee soon? I would dearly like to see you again." *I was so hoping he might say that.* "Yes, OK, it would be nice to see you again. If convenient perhaps we could meet next Wednesday as I finish at 12 noon. I work in Canterbury but I'm not sure how far it is from where you are, there's a Costa coffee bar next to M&S in the town centre, I could meet you there, say at 12.30 if that's good with you?"

"That's no problem and thank you. I'll let you get on with your shopping and look forward to seeing you this coming Wednesday." A few moments ago, I was stuck in a rut and thought my life was shit. That one phone call has now made me feel on top of the world. I know I'm only meeting up for a coffee but it just feels like a new chapter has opened in my life.

Over the weekend, I spent some time down at the stables with my horse and went for a ride. I'm so pleased he's settled in nicely in his new home.

It was Sunday evening and I needed to sort out what I was going to wear for work tomorrow but before that I'm going to ring my best friend Samantha and tell her the latest.

"Hi Samantha, you'll never guess who I got a call from yesterday."

She started giggling. "Well as you're the hottest single lady in town I can't even begin to imagine."

"It was only Captain Phillips, you know the guy I spoke to you about, the one who introduced himself at the engagement party of a college friend? He asked if I would like to meet up for a coffee, I wasn't that bothered but thought *why not*? It's a free coffee."

I could hear her laughing aloud. "You little liar, I bet you said yes before he'd even finished asking." I could hardly speak for giggling.

"Yes, you're so right. He's gorgeous, all six foot six of him. We're meeting up this Wednesday at the coffee shop in town and no you're not invited."

"You're such a spoil sport but promise me

you'll let me know how you got on."

"Yes, I promise but right now I've got to get my things ready for work so I'll speak to you later." After our chat, I had a shower and decided to have an early night.

I couldn't believe it was Wednesday already. I was feeling both excited and nervous about meeting up with Andrew at lunch time. I've decided to wear my smart trouser suit with matching shoes and not to overdo the makeup.

Having arrived at the office I was informed that one of my clients had to re- appoint due to ill health thus giving me the opportunity to catch up on some overdue paperwork.

I couldn't have timed it better, I was all done with fifteen minutes to spare but before setting off I popped into the ladies to powder my nose. Now refreshed I made my way to the coffee bar. Although excited I tried to stay calm and composed. As I entered the bar I could see Andrew sitting in the far corner. He came straight over to greet me.

"Hello Jane so lovely to see you, I've got a seat over here." With that deep rich sexy voice, I got instant butterflies in my stomach as I followed him across the room to where he was seated.

"Now what can I get you?"

"I'll have a latte please." I sat down at the table and waited for him to get the drinks.

"Here we are then two nice coffees." He sat down and looked over to me.

"Well Jane I have to confess I've secretly been looking forward to seeing you today. So, what are you doing with yourself?" If only he knew how excited I was to see him but I didn't want him to think that I was coming on to him. "Well, being a lawyer I practice at a local solicitor partnership here in Canterbury."

He sat back in his chair and smiled. "Not only are you a very attractive but also highly intelligent and I have nothing but total admiration for you."

"Well thank you Andrew. So, what's been happening in your life?"

"I'm on two weeks leave now then following my recent promotion I will be taking on my new role as Commander in Chief at the air base in Lincoln. I'll be ensuring the correct training is given to all pilots flying the latest air craft and the use of their sophisticated weaponry, a challenge that I'm very much looking forward to." *And he thinks I'm clever.* "Now that's enough of work. I would rather talk about you. I don't wish to dwell on the past but I think you are extremely brave and courageous to have endured what must have been a terrifying experience. When I last saw you at the engagement party I felt that something may have been troubling you but I felt it inappropriate to ask. I could never have imagined the physical abuse you suffered at the hands of such an evil man."

"Yes, it was not the best time in my life. The coroner's report stated that both the driver caused deaths, with the verdict of undue care and attention. While considering the way, their clothes were arranged on impact some form of sexual activity was taking place and no other parties were involved in the accident. As far as I'm concerned justice has been done and now I'm free to move on with my life."

"Well I'm so pleased that you're now focused on something positive with your career which I'm sure can be quite challenging. Now there is something that I must confess. I know things must still be a little raw and you must surely need more time to overcome this dreadful experience but I must confess from the very first moment I saw you and even before we spoke there was something magical about you that attracted me to you. When we danced together I truly didn't want the music to end. Then some few months later by sheer coincidence we came together at our friends' engagement. I so wanted to approach you but since you were married it would not have been the honourable thing to do. I still very much enjoyed the brief time spent in your company, but when leaving that evening I had to put on a brave face as I felt a great sadness that I may never see you again. So please forgive me if I may sound a little forward but perhaps you may consider joining me for dinner one evening. I perfectly understand if you decline but would very much enjoy the pleasure of your company."

I'm not ashamed to admit that I felt the same way towards him. "Yes Andrew, I would very much like to have dinner with you and thank you for asking. It is something I will very much look forward to."

His stern face turned into a huge smile. "Jane, you have just made me the happiest man ever. This is an occasion I could have only dreamed of just a few months ago,"

I had to smile as he looked like a cat that had the cream but in truth so did I. "Well Andrew, as much as I'm enjoying this coffee break I have to get back as I've got a client to see in one hour and have some paperwork to prepare beforehand." I would have liked to spend the rest of the day with him.

"Please don't let me keep you. Once again it is so nice to see you and if it's ok perhaps I may ring you this evening to arrange a suitable time for our evening meal."

"Yes, that would be fine. Thank you for the coffee and I'll look forward to speaking to you later." I left the coffee bar and made my way back to the office. I felt on such a high at the thought of going on a dinner date with this gorgeous man.

True to his word Andrew rang and we arranged to go out this coming Saturday. The first thing I had to do was to treat myself to a new dress as this was going to be one very special date. After getting comfortable for the night I rang my best friend Samantha.

"Hi, I thought it was time I gave you a ring to catch up. How are things with you?"

"Hi Jane lovely to hear from you, I hope you're well and everything is good. How's your new venture in the legal department going? I bet it's keeping you busy."

"Yes, things are going well. It's nice to have something to focus on and I'm feeling a lot more confident." *She could never know just how good I'm feeling right now.* "Well you certainly sound happy and I'm so pleased for you. How about we meet up for a coffee? It seems ages since we last met up. You can tell me all about your new venture."

"That will be great but there's something I've

just got to tell you before then. Guess who is taking me out for dinner this Saturday evening?" *She's going to be so surprised.*

"I couldn't even begin to guess, so come on then who's the lucky man?" *Who's the lucky man? More like who's the lucky woman.*

"Well it's none other than Captain Phillips who I mentioned wanted to meet for a coffee this lunch time and before leaving he asked me if I would like to join him for an evening meal."

I could hear her gasping for breath down the phone. "You do realise your dating the most desirable and eligible bachelor on this planet and will be the envy of all women including myself? You lucky, lucky bitch and I mean that in the nicest possible way. That is so amazing and I'm so pleased for you. As far as I'm concerned, he's made the perfect choice.

"Thank you, Samantha. I can't believe it myself and I'm so looking forward to it."

"Well you go and enjoy yourself and have a wonderful time as there's no one that deserves it more than you, so how about we meet up for a coffee sometime next week and you can tell me all about it?"

"Ok that will be great, I'll look forward to it."

We had a chat for a few moments longer and arranged to meet up Monday for lunch.

Chapter Fifteen

It was Saturday morning and I was in town searching for something to wear tonight as I wanted to look my very best. After a few hours of searching I found and bought a beautiful red dress and shoes to match. They were very expensive but what? It was well worth it just for the feel-good factor and much needed self-esteem boost. After browsing around a few more shops I made my way back home as I had to wash my hair before getting ready.

I had just half an hour to finish getting ready. Even though he is not here anymore I still feel nervous when putting on my red lipstick and have flash backs of being punched and having it drawn all over my face by that bastard.

With just a few minutes to spare and one final look in the mirror I was ready to go. I just hoped he would like the way I look. I jumped as the intercom buzzer sounded and I nervously pressed the button and spoke, "Hello?"

"Hi Jane," Just the sound of his voice made me all a tremble.

"Hi Andrew, just have to get my bag and I'll be right down." I picked up my bag and with just one final glance in the hall mirror made my way down to the front door. As I opened it there stood the most gorgeous immaculately dressed man with a smile displaying the most perfect set of white teeth.

"Hello Jane, are we ready for dinner?" Standing beside him I was ready for anything.

"Yes, have you got somewhere in mind?"

"Well although I've never eaten at this restaurant before it came highly recommended so I made a reservation for this evening and thought it would be nice to share the experience together. So, let's go and find out." As we walked to his car the smell of his aftershave or whatever he was wearing sent my hormones racing.

After about half an hour's drive we arrived at a very smart looking restaurant set in the country side. As we made our way to the entrance a member of staff greeted us. Once we confirmed our booking he escorted us to our table that was set in the far corner situated in a bay window. It was just perfect. The waiter came over and gave us each a wine list and menu.

After placing our order the waiter returned with a bottle of wine and poured a small amount for us to taste. On approval, he filled both glasses.

Andrew raised his glass and leaned forward towards me. "Here's to a lovely evening." I raised my glass and we both touched them together.

"Yes, and thank you for inviting me, it really is a beautiful place."

As we replaced our glasses he considered my eyes. "Jane, you look absolutely stunning and have to confess that I feel so very lucky and proud to be sharing your company." I just feel on top of the world. I'm sitting here in this beautiful restaurant having a romantic meal with the most gorgeous man on the planet, and he says he's lucky.

"Thank you, Andrew, that was a nice thing to say. I too was looking forward to meeting up with you again." As I spoke the waiter placed our meals on the table.

After a beautiful meal and talking to Andrew, sadly the evening ended and it was time to leave. On arriving back to my plaice Andrew escorted me to the door.

Towering over me, he leaned forwards and spoke in a soft tone, "Thank you for a most enjoyable evening. May I be so bold as to ask if we may see each other again?" I felt weak at the knees at the very thought of it.

"Yes, that would be nice. Tonight, has been wonderful and thank you. Perhaps you might ring me later in the week." He gave a big gorgeous smile.

"You can't imagine how good that's made me feel. Now I've kept you long enough, I will bid you a very good night and will be in touch really soon." Before leaving he leant forward and gently kissed me on the lips. What with the smell of his after shave and his lips touching mine I so wanted more, but as frustrating as it was he remained the perfect gentleman?

Over the next nine months we saw each other on a regular basis and gradually became an item. I am absolutely besotted and simply adore everything about him, and he in turn expressed his deep love for me. Being such a true gentleman he gave me all the time I needed to overcome the past. We had only ever embraced and kissed but not been fully intimate. Then one evening while having dinner he reached out his hand and held mine. On this evening, he seemed a bit nervous as he began to speak, "Jane, I hope you don't think of me as being presumptuous or forward but there is something I wish to ask you." Suddenly I felt vulnerable and insecure. Is he about to end our relationship? I could feel his hand tighten on mine as he spoke.

"I'm sure you now know how much I deeply love and care for you and we have shared many precious times together. But I was wondering if you would like to share a romantic weekend in Paris with me, just the two of us." I could feel myself welling up and trying hard not to cry. It had been nine months since that dreadful experience but the past was now well and truly behind me. I was now ready and looking forward to being in a full relationship with the man I truly love.

"Andrew, I love you so much and this feeling can't be wrong. Yes, I would love to come to Paris with you and know it will be just wonderful." I could sense him relax as he leaned forward to give me a kiss.

"Jane, you are amazing, nine months ago, I was leading a somewhat mundane life and now I feel like a million dollars and the luckiest man alive."

Chapter Sixteen

Two weeks on we're boarding a plane to Paris I can't even begin to say how excited I am and I keep having to pinch myself to make sure it's for real and not just a dream. After a short flight, we landed in Paris and were taken by taxi to our hotel. On arrival, we were greeted by a very smartly dressed door man who took in our luggage. We entered this huge marble reception area where we checked in then escorted to our room. It was breath-taking on the top floor overlooking the Eiffel Tower and leading off from the lounge was the bedroom with stunning views over Paris. Inside was the biggest bed I'd ever seen with silk sheets. My heart began to flutter and I felt both nervous and excited as I knew we were going to make love in this very bed tonight.

Andrew gave the doorman a tip as he left then came over to me and gave me a kiss.

"So, what do you think, is it what you expected?"

"It is absolutely beautiful and with such amazing views. You've spoiled me like you always do. It's just perfect." This place must have cost a fortune; I've never seen such luxury.

"I'm so glad you like it. May I suggest before we unpack we look at some of the sights and have a bit of lunch? As a surprise, I've booked a candle lit dinner tonight on a river boat so we can enjoy the sights of the city." I went up to him and gave him a big hug and a kiss.

After taking a walk around the city we stopped for a light lunch in one of the many street bars. We sat outside and found it quite interesting just people watching.

Back at the hotel we unpacked a few things but as there were only a couple of hours before going out this evening it was time to think about getting ready. As I was sorting out my clothes Andrew came in the bedroom.

"As it's time to get ready, I'm going to take a shower and get changed in the bathroom across from the lounge leaving you to get ready here in the bedroom and end suite. I promise I won't intrude on your privacy." That was very considerate as I would have felt a bit uncomfortable taking a shower while he was in the near vicinity. He gave me a gentle kiss and left the room. To feel totally at ease, I gently and quietly turned the lock on the door. I knew he wouldn't come in but I now felt relaxed having the freedom of movement to get ready and look my best for him.

After a shower, I sat at this beautiful marble dressing table. Happy with the way I looked, I put on my new red dress that I had bought especially for the occasion. It fits perfectly and looked nice showing just enough cleavage without looking tarty. After putting on my new matching shoes, a bit of jewellery and a spray of perfume I was ready. Nervously I opened the door and went into the lounge where Andrew was sitting and reading. He got up from his chair and came over towards me, immaculately dressed and wearing a light pin striped suit and a waist coat. *He is just so bloody handsome and I still find it hard to believe I'm here in Paris with him for a romantic weekend.*

"Wow, you look absolutely stunning. What have I done to deserve such a beautiful woman?" I looked up at him and smiled.

"Thank you but I have to say that you scrub up well yourself." We both started laughing and he gave me a kiss on the cheek.

"Well I've got a taxi waiting downstairs to take us to the river boat so if you're ready let's go and enjoy the evening." We took the lift down to the reception hall and went outside to the awaiting taxi. As we arrived the riverboat looked spectacular. It was all lit up with lights reflecting on the water. We were greeted on board by a very smartly dressed guide who escorted us to our candle lit table overlooking the river. The boat was fully booked and once everyone had arrived and was seated you could hear the boat's engine as we slowly started to move out into the river. Once moving everyone was given a complimentary glass of champagne. It was so romantic cruising on the river looking at all the city lights. It was just like a fairy tale come true. Then only a short moment later the waiter was at the table with our meals.

As we were about to start Andrew reached out his hand and placed it in mine. "Being with you Jane is a very special time in my life. I am so proud and happy that you wish to share this time with me. All I care about is your happiness and never ever wish to see sadness in your eyes again. You are so precious and I love you more than words could ever say."

Feeling overwhelmed, I could feel a tear trickle down my cheek. "That is such a beautiful thing to say. I too love you so much and tonight will forever stay in my heart as a moment I will treasure forever."

"Thank you, Jane. I can't begin to tell you how much those words mean to me." He started to smile as he released his hand. "So, let's enjoy our meal and the views of this lovely city."

This was the most beautiful romantic experience of my life but sadly after about a two hour round trip the river boat was back to where we started. The skipper thanked everyone as we disembarked and made our way out. Our taxi was waiting and after a short drive we were back at the hotel. After tipping the driver we went to the reception hall and took the lift to our room. On entering there on the table was a huge beautiful bouquet of red roses with a card that read 'For a very special lady who I simply love and adore.' I went over and gave him a kiss.

"Thank you, they're absolutely beautiful." I was so overwhelmed and I just wanted him there and then. He must have had the very same feelings as we held hands and went into the bedroom. He closed the door behind us and dimmed the lights then leaned towards me. Our lips touched as we embraced and kissed passionately. I've waited so long for this moment and I know tonight is going to be the perfect time.

He gently began to remove my garments and I in turn removed his. He lay my naked body onto the bed and began to pleasure me in a way I never thought possible. My body was screaming out for him but I so wanted to please him as well. Slowly moving down his magnificent body I began to do what just came so naturally. After a few moments, he knelt before me; the moment I have been so longing for was now here. His erection gently but firmly entered my eagerly awaiting body. We are now as one and every nerve ending in my body was tingling with utter desire as we moved in unison together. I never wanted this to end but try as I may I couldn't control myself any longer. I cried out and my entire body erupted as he brought me to a mind-blowing orgasm and what made it even more beautiful was at that very moment I felt him climax deep inside me. This special intimate moment we had just shared was not about sex but about the true meaning of making love the way I always dreamt it should be. I just didn't want the night to end.

We woke the next morning still in each other's arms. Andrew gave me a gentle kiss that turned into a bigger kiss and before long we were making passionate love again in this beautiful king size bed. What a lovely feeling and an amazing weekend, one I shall truly treasure for the rest of my life.

After breakfast, we packed our things as sadly it was time to leave for the airport. Before we left Andrew sat me down and leaned towards me and spoke in a soft tone, "I just want to say thank you for the most beautiful time in my life and how much I love you. I feel the luckiest man alive to be with someone so special."

I felt myself welling up as I embraced him. "Thank you, Andrew, it's been the most amazing experience ever. I've never been treated like a lady before and I'm over whelmed by how you make me feel. No words could ever express how much I love you." After a nice cuddle and kiss we left the hotel and departed to the airport. What a weekend to remember.

Chapter Seventeen

Once home I rang my best friend and arranged to meet up for a coffee as I knew she would be bursting to know how I got on.

Being in love and having someone love and care for you is the most wonderful emotional experience ever. Andrew and I see each other two or three times a week and after a few months he suggested we have dinner at the restaurant where we had our first date together. Of course, I said yes and that I would very much look forward to it as it would be nice to reminisce.

After getting ready the following evening Andrew came around and picked me up. As we got in the car he turned towards me, "I don't know about you but this takes me back to our first date and I can't help feeling a little nervous and exited."

I leaned forward and gave him a kiss. "Yes, I know what you mean but it's a nice feeling especially as we both feel the same." We drove off to the restaurant, on our arrival we were shown to the same table we shared on our first date. Placed on it was a red rose; he is such a wonderful romantic. He leaned forward and held my hand.

"This brings back such happy memories. I pre-booked this table as I wanted it to feel the same as on our first evening together." We both smiled as we considered each other's eyes. Then the waiter spoiled it by bringing over the menus and wine list.

After ordering our meals the waiter bought over a bottle of wine and after approval he poured out two glasses. Looking across the table, I still find it hard to believe that this most gorgeous man is in love with me.

On finishing our meal Andrew put the plates to one side and then reached out holding my hands. As he started to speak there was a distinct tremor in his voice. "Jayne my dearest, you are so very special and as you may gather I love you most dearly. At this very moment, I've never felt so nervous but there's something I have to ask of you." He put his hand in his pocket and pulled out a small velvet box and when opened it displayed the most beautiful diamond ring I've ever laid eyes on.

"Will you marry me and do me the great honour of becoming my wife?" I just burst into tears. Never in my wildest dreams could I have ever imagined that my life would turn around with such fulfilment and happiness.

I considered his dark brown eyes. "Yes of course and I would be so proud to do so."

He leaned over and gave me a great big kiss then summoned over the waiter.

"We have a celebration to make. Would you please bring over a bottle of champagne and two fresh glasses?" We made a toast to each other, pledging our love and new life together.

On leaving the restaurant Andrew took me back to my place and we kissed goodnight. I knew it was a bit late but I was so excited I had to ring my best friend and tell her the good news. I hoped she hadn't gone to bed.

"Hi Samantha, I hope I haven't disturbed you."

"No, I was just getting ready to turn in for the night. Is everything ok?"

"Yes, you could say that. I know we're meeting for coffee the day after tomorrow but this can't wait."

"Calm down, are you in some kind or trouble?"

"Of course, everything is fine. I've just been out for dinner with Andrew. It was the same place where we had our first romantic evening together. Then after our meal he held my hand and proposed. He's only asked me to marry him and of course I said yes! Then he slipped the most beautiful diamond ring on my finger that I've ever seen." I could hear Samantha scream out in excitement.

"Wow, that is just so amazing, I'm just so happy for you and can't stop crying but they're tears of absolute joy. If there's anybody in this world that deserves to be happy it's you Jane. Plus, I've now got a good excuse to buy a new hat." I knew Samantha would share my excitement and after a long girly chat I took myself off to bed. I hoped that when I awoke in the morning everything wouldn't just be a dream. Tomorrow I'm going over to my parents and tell them the good news as I knew they will be thrilled at the prospect of me marrying Andrew.

After two months of preparation we decided on a modest wedding with just family and close friends. The big day had arrived and the car is now on its way to the church. My father was waiting to escort me down the aisle. The traditional wedding theme began to play as my father and I slowly walked towards where my tall handsome soon-to-be husband was waiting.

It was a very special happy and emotional day and after the reception we said our goodbyes before setting off on our honey moon.

Two years on we're the proud parents of our gorgeous one year old son and recently arrived beautiful baby daughter. Looking back, it's hard to imagine that my life was at such an all-time low and not worth living, then from out of nowhere from just a chance meeting, the man who I was destined to love and be with was there patiently waiting for me. *Thank you, George, your premonition was right*

Should anyone ever ask what my favourite dance would be? I think they would be most surprised when I say, "The Excuse Me Waltz."

THE END

For updates about current and upcoming releases together with exclusive promotions and your Free Downloads, please visit the author's Book Store at:
http://www.jkashley.com/

19546586R00099

Printed in Great Britain
by Amazon